The Tides Between Us

USA TODAY BEST SELLING AUTHOR

CALI MELLE

Editor: Rumi Khan

Cover Design: Cat Imb, TRC Designs by Cat

Proofreader: Alexandra Cowell

Sensitivity Readers: Cat Wilkinson and Honey

PLAYLIST

ALONE WITH YOU - ALINA BARAZ

CARDIGAN - TAYLOR SWIFT

LOWER EAST SIDE - RILEY

ONE WAY - 6LACK, T-PAIN

WANT U AROUND - OMAR APOLLO, RUEL

CONVERSATIONS IN THE DARK - JOHN LEGEND

FRESH EYES - ANDY GRAMMER

A LACK OF COLOR - DEATH CAB FOR CUTIE

PRETTY LITTLE FEARS - 6LACK, J. COLE

HOW DOES IT FEEL - SYDNY AUGUST

LA DON'T LOOK GOOD ON U - ASTN

ALL TO YOU - RUSS, KIANA LEDE

This one is for the girlies who love a cinnamon roll hero with a filthy mouth. Bonus points for him if he also happens to save sea turtles.

CHAPTER ONE
DECLAN

The lower half of my legs were submerged in the ocean as I floated in the water, just past the coastline where the waves break. It wasn't a good morning for surfing and the East Coast was nothing like the West when it came to their swells. The ocean gods weren't paying me any favors this morning, but I technically wasn't supposed to be surfing anyway.

At least the sunrise didn't disappoint.

I turned myself around on my board and watched the sky as it began to shift through a series of hues of color. The pinks transformed into yellow and orange, mixing together as the sun began to crest the horizon. It was quiet and peaceful. The ocean had a way of calming my soul.

Sunrise was always my favorite part of the day. The

rest of the world was still waking up, but out here, the ocean was always full of life. Dolphin fins bobbed above the surface and a few jumped into the air. The sun poked up above the horizon and it cast its light across the ripples, creating a shimmering essence across the water. My eyelids fluttered shut and I inhaled deeply, filling my lungs with the salt-tinged air.

This was where I belonged.

I stayed out on the water until the sky had shifted into a bright blue, showcasing the sun. There wasn't a single cloud in sight. Rolling onto my stomach, I used my good arm to paddle until I met the waves and let them push me closer to the shore. Submerging both of my arms into the ocean, I gave one forceful push, feeling the twinge of pain in my left shoulder before I was able to hop off my board and carry it in.

A dislocated shoulder wasn't a death sentence. It wouldn't take surfing away from me, but it was undoubtedly an inconvenience. A month ago, I was at the Oahu Pro Classic in Hawaii. The water was choppy as hell as a storm was rolling in. I lost my balance while tube riding. The barreling wave was absolute perfection, but I slipped and tumbled into the water. My shoulder was pulled from its socket as the ocean tossed me around a bit.

It hurt like a bitch, but nothing compared to the feeling of when the doctor popped it back in place. When I got back to Malibu, they told me my recovery would be three to four months. It wasn't ideal, but it wasn't the end of the world. I took the next flight out to Florida to bunker down with my brother in Orchid City. The waves were shit here and it wouldn't be as tempting and dangerous if I decided to hop on my board earlier than I was supposed to. The physical therapist I had been working with here was hopeful I would be looking at closer to twelve weeks rather than the full sixteen.

My feet sank into the sand as I walked to the shore. The granules scratched at my skin and I welcomed the feeling. I walked a few feet away from where the water met the beach and I turned once more to look back at the ocean. It was killing me to not be out there like I was used to, but I knew I had to be patient. I could not afford to fuck this up.

Something dark and peculiar caught my eye. At first glance, it looked like a horseshoe crab that had washed up, but the shape was different and it wasn't black. I propped my board up in the sand and began to walk over to investigate. I squinted my eyes to get a better look as I closed the distance between myself and the object. There were streaks of bright red washing into the water.

As I got closer, I realized what I was looking at. I noticed the muddy-colored shell immediately, followed by the block-shaped head of the turtle. I didn't know much about turtles, but this one's shell was only about a foot and a half in diameter. Based on the way it looked, I figured it was a loggerhead, which was particularly common in this area. Growing up by the ocean, you quickly learned about the environment and the inhabitants of it.

My eyes traveled from the streaks of blood to the turtle as I began to scan it from a bit of a distance. It stared up at me with fright, but the pain was evident. It didn't even attempt to move away from me as it stayed exactly where it had washed up. As my gaze reached its front legs, I noticed there was fishing wire wrapped tightly around it, cutting through its flesh.

The damned thing was injured and it needed help.

Typically, you were supposed to call a hotline for someone to come pick the animal up, but as I watched the blood mix with the salty ocean water, I knew I couldn't just wait here with the turtle in hopes that someone would eventually arrive. A sigh escaped me and I shook my head momentarily before sliding my hands beneath the turtle and lifting it into the air.

It was almost as if the thing was paralyzed by fear, or perhaps the pain. Whatever it was, it didn't fight against me or try to escape. There was a facility less than a mile away. I just needed to get the turtle into the back of my Jeep and get it there.

"It's okay, dude," I told the turtle, like it had any understanding of English. My feet kicked up sand as I lengthened my strides while walking toward the road. "I'm gonna get you some help."

It was a short walk to the car and my shoulder was throbbing by the time I reached it. I laid down a towel and loaded the turtle into the trunk like it was completely normal. We stared at one another for a few moments before I shook my head to myself. What the hell was I doing?

I quickly sprinted back to the beach to grab my board and ran back to the Jeep. The turtle was in the same spot I left it and I strapped my surfboard to the roof before hopping in behind the wheel. Dust kicked up from the tires as I shifted into first gear and let off the clutch while pulling onto the road. I was careful while driving for the turtle's sake, but I needed to get it to the rehabilitation facility as quickly as I could.

It was less than a three-minute drive. The sign was just along the side of the road. *Orchid City Marine Research & Rehabilitation Center.* I pulled my car down the long winding drive that led to the main building. There were four smaller buildings that I could see, scattered behind the main entrance. I stopped directly out front, not bothering to park in a parking spot.

I threw the vehicle in park, killed the engine, and hopped out before rushing around to the back of the Jeep. Part of the towel underneath the turtle's flipper was saturated with blood, but it appeared to have slowed down a bit. Using the towel to cradle the turtle, I lifted it into the air and removed it from my trunk. My movements were hesitant as I carried it to the front door, careful to not jar it at all.

The glass doors slid open as I stepped in front of them and a rush of cold air wrapped itself around me. It was quiet inside and my flip-flops were loud, echoing throughout the space as they slapped the linoleum floor. There was a woman with her back turned to me, but she didn't turn around as I walked up to the front desk area. I set the turtle down on the floor by my feet and stared at the back of her head.

Her long midnight hair was pulled back in a pony-tail and she was filling up some syringes with liquid. I shifted my weight on my feet, my eyes scanning the curves of her body before landing on the back of her head once again.

"Excuse me," I said after a few more moments of silence passed. She didn't turn to face me and I was growing impatient. The damn turtle was still bleeding and this woman was acting like I wasn't even here. She turned her head slightly, but still didn't acknowledge me. I watched her jaw move as she was chewing something and I saw the opened strawberry Pop-Tart wrapper beside her. "Hello?" I said louder this time.

She was arranging the syringes in a tray and my eyebrows were pulled together as I gave the back of her head a perplexed look. I was extremely confused why she was ignoring me. A sigh escaped me and I moved around to the side of the desk until I was about to step behind it. She must have caught sight of me from the corner of her eye. She whipped her head to the side, her lips parting slightly as her bright blue eyes widened.

Holy shit. My breath caught in my throat and I was instantly captivated by her. Her features were completely symmetrical and my eyes traveled across the planes of her face. Her cheekbones were high and prominent, her nose perfectly straight. For a moment, I forgot what I was even doing here.

She smiled brightly at me and her eyes were warm and welcoming. I couldn't fucking breathe.

"I brought a turtle," I said in a hurry as I ran an anxious hand through my tousled waves. My hair was still damp from the ocean and I pushed the locks away from my face. I instantly wanted to take the words back as I realized how stupid they sounded. "I found an injured turtle on the beach and I brought it in."

She moved her hands, twisting them around with her arms as she moved her fingers. Her lips moved simultaneously; however, she remained silent. The dots connected and it clicked in my brain. She wasn't ignoring me. She didn't even know I was there talking to her because she couldn't hear me.

I tilted my head to the side as I tried to read her lips, but quickly realized how terrible I was at it. Realization struck her and her face faltered slightly. She shook her head apologetically and picked up a notepad beside her. Her hand moved quickly as she wrote on the paper.

Where is the turtle? How badly is it injured?

I looked at the paper and went to reach for it to write back to her. Her bright blue eyes met mine as she shook her head again and wrote something else down.

I can read lips.

I nodded. "It's over here," I motioned to the side of me. "There's wire wrapped around its flipper and it was bleeding on the beach. I know we're supposed to call stuff like this in, but I couldn't just leave it on the beach to potentially bleed out."

She followed me around to the front of the desk area and crouched down as she inspected the turtle. Silence settled between us, although there was some sense of comfort in it. She held her finger up to me before she scooped the turtle up and rushed through one of the doors behind the desk.

Curiosity got the better of me. I followed after her, stepping back into the hospital area of the facility. She was a few strides ahead of me and I watched her as she ducked into another room. I stopped just inside the doorway as she set the turtle down on a metal table. Two people in scrubs were instantly looking at it, signing questions to her, and she signed back to answer.

The one guy who was looking at the turtle's flipper caught sight of me and lifted his gaze to mine. He nodded his head and the woman spun on her heel to face me. I watched as she signed something to the other staff members once more before marching toward me. Her palm was soft and her hand was small as she wrapped it around my wrist. She walked past me, turning me around with her as she led me back toward the lobby.

I couldn't fight the smile on my lips.

She didn't stop until we reached the front desk and she was grabbing for the notepad and pen again.

You can't be back there. It's for staff only.

I shrugged with indifference. "What about the turtle? Will you guys be able to help it?"

She nodded before scribbling another note on the piece of paper.

We won't know for sure, but it definitely could have been worse. That turtle is lucky you found her when you did.

"Pop-Tart," I said abruptly, which had her giving me a quizzical look. "Her name is Pop-Tart."

You named her?

I shrugged again. "It felt like she needed a name instead of just referring to her as 'that turtle'. Don't you guys name the animals anyways?"

She smiled brightly and nodded.

We do. Pop-Tart sounds like the perfect name for her.

"When will you know more about what will happen with her?"

I watched her delicate hand as she began to write something again. I was officially invested in this turtle's recovery and I wanted an excuse to see her again.

Check back in a few days. We should have more concrete information then.

"Perfect, I'll check back in then." I smiled back at her. "I didn't get your name."

She raised an eyebrow and wrote it down.

Giana.

"Declan." I held my hand out to her. "Have a good rest of your day, Giana."

My eyes lingered on her face a moment longer and

silence settled between us as she offered me a smile and a nod. I loved the way her name felt rolling off my tongue. I left her without another word.

I was a patient man.

I could wait a few days before seeing Giana again.

CHAPTER TWO
GIANA

I stared at the door he had just disappeared through. My heart pounded in my chest and I tried to regain my composure. He was a pleasant surprise this morning. Most people who dropped off animals or called us to come pick them up were never concerned with their rehabilitation process. There was a part of me that knew he probably didn't really care but was just trying to be polite.

Whether he came back again or not, he was already imprinted in my memory and I would gladly store him there. His skin was sun-kissed. His hair was a light shade of brown that shimmered with natural highlights in his tousled waves. He was wearing a pair of board shorts and a tank top that revealed his muscular arms.

I had spent enough time around the ocean that I knew a surfer when I saw one.

He wasn't what I needed to be focusing on,

although he had really caught my attention. I returned back to the syringes that I was filling with medications for some of our turtles. After grabbing them, I headed over to the one building that housed about fifteen pools for some of the different animals and began to give the medication to the ones that needed it.

The facility was world renowned. Most of the animals that we rehabilitated were all native to Florida, but occasionally we would get one transported in from other states along the East Coast. We had a hospital, research center, and a rehabilitation section. It was quite impressive and I was working my dream job here.

I finished up with the medication rounds I had been assigned to before returning back to the main building. After cleaning everything up, I headed back to the room where the turtle was that the surfer guy had brought in. Pop-Tart, he decided to name her. It was peculiar, but who was I to judge?

Crew lifted his head as I stepped into the room and nodded to me. He was our head veterinarian here. I worked more on the research side as a marine biologist, but we were down a few vet techs, so I helped out wherever they needed me. Miranda moved beside him as she arranged some different supplies.

"How are things looking with her?" I signed to him as he stood up straight.

"We're going to need to do surgery to repair her flipper, but I'm fairly confident we will be able to fix it well enough

that she can be rereleased. We will have to wait until we see how surgery and recovery goes before determining that."

I smiled at him. That was great news. Sometimes the damage was too extensive to the animals we got here and we weren't able to rerelease them into the wild. Hearing we would hopefully be able to return her to her natural habitat was amazing news.

"That's great," I signed to him as I looked at Miranda while she began to prep Pop-Tart for surgery. *"Is there anything I can do while the two of you start Pop-Tart's surgery?"*

Crew's forehead creased. "Pop-Tart?" he spoke aloud while signing. "Who decided on that for her name?"

"The guy who dropped her off named her before he left."

Miranda smiled and Crew gave me a look of curiosity. "Interesting."

"Can you check the dolphin pool?" I read Miranda's lips as she spoke. She wasn't as good with ASL like Crew was. "There's a list of some things that needed to be done. Shaina should be coming in around ten and I think Dominick was coming in this afternoon."

I nodded my head. *"Yep. Good luck with surgery and keep me updated."*

"Will do," Crew signed back to me before the two of them directed their attention back to Pop-Tart. I excused myself from the room without another word and settled back into the silence that had always enveloped me.

There was a sense of solitude and comfort that came

with the silence. There were also times where I couldn't help but feel like I was alone in the world. I knew I wasn't. I lost my hearing when I was eight, so I've spent most of my life not being able to hear. It honestly felt like a distant memory now, but it still lingered.

I gave up the thoughts long ago about wishing I could hear again. Instead, I was just left with being able to hear my own thoughts or the sounds inside my dreams. I still dreamt with sound. Because I had lost my hearing during late childhood, it was possible for me to dream that way.

When I was a child, I ended up severely sick with influenza. It ended up affecting my heart, which had me hospitalized for quite some time. The doctors had me on crazy amounts of medication, which had an adverse reaction that had actually caused permanent hearing loss. It was frightening as a child, but my family was always supportive.

My parents and my brother and I all learned sign language together. It was the biggest blessing in my life. I had a way to communicate with people. And then when other people in my life made the effort to learn how to communicate with me, it showed how kind-hearted some could really be. Instead of being dismissive, they made accommodations for me.

I headed over to the building that had a massive pool inside that housed some of the dolphins we had. I went through Miranda's list and the other odd things she had listed until Shaina came in and took over.

After handing everything over to her, I locked myself away in my lab for the rest of the day. We had a few turtles come in recently that we had quarantined because of an infection. I was doing research as it was a different variation than the one we were used to seeing. I took a quick break for lunch before burying myself back in my work.

As the day grew closer to an end, my phone vibrated from where it was sitting on my desk and I grabbed it to check. A text message popped up from my best friend Winter. We had a group chat with her and I and my brother's girlfriend, Harper.

WINTER

We're still on for girls' night tonight, right?

HARPER

Absolutely. There's this new restaurant Nico was talking about that I think we should try out. It's called Botanics.

I was so thankful for the two of them. Winter and I had been friends since we were kids as we had both grown up in Orchid City together. We grew apart for a few years when she left for Vermont for college, but since she moved back home, we picked up like we never lost time.

Harper was the best thing that could have possibly happened to my brother and she was one of the sweetest people I had ever met. Our mother passed away a few years ago and Nico really struggled after her passing. He never fully got over it, but Harper brought a new light into his life. He had fallen into the habit of being quite the playboy before she showed up. Their relationship was actually quite sweet and I loved seeing my brother happy.

GIANA

What time did you guys want to meet there?

WINTER

How about seven?

HARPER

That works for me.

GIANA

I'll meet you guys there.

I put my phone on Do Not Disturb mode so I could finish up my work before heading home to get ready to go meet them. My new apartment wasn't far from my workplace and it was very close to the ocean. I personally loved it. I had the best view for sunrises.

When my mother was first diagnosed, she and my father moved to Tampa for her to get treatment there. I moved with them and stayed after she passed because I hated seeing our father so devastated. Nico was busy with hockey and I didn't expect him to put everything in his life to the side to care for our father. But our father was a lost man. When our mother died, a big chunk of him died alongside her.

I ended up moving back to Orchid City with my brother until I was able to get my own place. Now I was back on my own, thriving alone. It was the way I preferred it. Nico didn't talk to our father often and my contact with him was minimal but I still tried to check in with him every once in a while.

In my eyes, no one deserved to be alone. But I think that was what our father preferred. He loved Nico and I equally. We just never came close to the love he had for our mother. She was the light of his life. Hell, she was the light of all of our lives. I liked to think she was looking down on me, proud of everything I was doing.

And every time I stepped out into the sunshine, it made me think of her. And I always thought of her with a smile on my face.

———

Winter and Harper were already waiting at the restaurant when I got there. It was like stepping into a magical garden. The entire ceiling was made of glass. Plants hung from beams above. There was an entire wall that was covered with flowers and different plants. It was one of the coolest places I had ever been to.

I saw the two of them seated at a table and headed over to them. They both smiled and waved to me as I sat down. Winter knew sign language from when we were kids and I lost my hearing. Harper had been learning from my brother since we met. It was nice having Winter here too, because she could translate if it was something Harper didn't fully understand.

We fell into an easy conversation about our days and work. Harper had her own photography business and was shooting a wedding this coming weekend. Winter was getting ready to go do some traveling with her boyfriend, Kai. He was a professional golfer and another lifelong friend. Although, he was moody and broody, except for when it came to Winter.

"How was your day, G?" Winter asked me after we ordered our drinks. Their cocktail menu here was all floral themed and I was excited for the hibiscus strawberry mojito I ordered.

"It was a pretty normal day," I signed to the two of them nonchalantly. *"Although, this morning was pretty interesting. This hot surfer dropped off an injured turtle he had found on the beach."*

Winter's and Harper's eyes lit up. "Please, do tell us more," Harper said with a mischievous smile as she propped her elbows on the table and rested her chin on top of her hands. "Did you get his name?"

I nodded. *"Declan,"* I signed to them.

Harper dropped her hands onto the table. "Like Declan Parks?"

Winter gave her a questioning look. "Who's that?"

"He's one of the best surfers in the world." She quickly reached for her purse and dug for her phone just as our server brought our drinks back. We all told her what we wanted, except I had to point to mine on the menu since most people I encountered didn't know sign language. Harper quickly typed something into her phone and then turned the screen to face me. "Is this your mystery turtle rescuer?"

I stared at the phone, looking at a picture of the same guy who I had met this morning. Butterfly wings scratched at the inside of my stomach as they fluttered. I pulled my lips in between my teeth and nodded. His bright white smile shined from the phone as he smiled at whoever took his picture.

"Do you know him?" Winter asked Harper as she set down her cocktail.

She shook her head. "When I worked as a sports photographer, there was always talk about different athletes that were blowing up at the time. I had heard of him before, although I never had the opportunity to take any pictures of him. He's fine as hell."

Even though Harper was dating my brother, it didn't bother me hearing her say that. She would never step out on my brother and it was hard to not appreciate the way someone like Declan Parks looked.

"He really is good-looking, Giana," Winter chimed in. "Did you get his number or anything like that?"

I gave them both an incredulous look. *"Um, no. He literally came in and dropped off the turtle. We talked briefly, exchanged names, and he said he would check back in a few days to see how the turtle was doing."*

The two of them smiled again and Harper laughed

as she shook her head. "Girl... he's coming back to check in on the *turtle*?"

"He's not just coming back for the turtle, G," Winter said with a wink. "He's coming back to see you too."

I shook my head at the two of them. *"You don't know that."*

"There's no way he's just coming to see how the turtle is doing," Harper said with an impish look in her eyes. "He wants to see you or he could easily call to check in on the turtle."

Winter nodded as Harper spoke. "Mark my words, babe. He's only going to show up when you're there because you got his attention."

Their words sank in and I couldn't help but feel those damn butterflies again. Declan had my attention and now I was intrigued. But I needed to make sure my curiosity didn't get the better of me.

I knew nothing about Declan Parks, but a part of me was hoping they were right.

Because I couldn't help but want to see him again too.

CHAPTER THREE
DECLAN

Sitting on the table at my physical therapist's office, I waited for him to come back with an ice pack. After going through the routine of strengthening exercises, there was always a cool-down period. I was situated on one of their tables and was required to ice my shoulder for fifteen minutes before I was cleared to go. My sessions were three times a week, plus the exercises I was supposed to be doing on my own. Three times a week for the next ten weeks.

Gabriel walked over with the ice pack and handed it to me before he left the room again. I was alone with my thoughts and as I iced my left shoulder, I couldn't stop my thoughts from drifting back to that damn turtle. Life was always a mystery, but it felt like Pop-Tart was sent to me from the ocean gods. Like a gift from the universe.

It felt so bizarre. I never was one to believe in coincidences. Things happened for a reason, regardless of what they were. It wasn't a simple coincidence that I found that turtle on the beach that morning. It wasn't a coincidence that I had injured my left shoulder and the turtle's left flipper was the one that was injured.

There were too many signs that were pointing in the direction of fate, but I wasn't sure what the endgame was for the universe. I was just simply along for the ride, although I found it peculiar and interesting that these little things were all setting up some definitive path.

I couldn't help but wonder if they had anything to do with the woman with hair as black as ink. There was no reason for her to be occupying the empty space in my brain, but I've been stuck on the thought of her since the other day. *Four days, to be exact.* I was genuinely curious and concerned about Pop-Tart's well-being, yet I couldn't help but want to head back to the marine center to see the ethereal goddess who entered my life that day.

Giana.

There was something about her that was captivating. I couldn't help but want to know more about her. Perhaps it was just my brain's way of finding and using anything it could find as a distraction. It was killing me, not being able to surf the swells like I was used to. I lived and breathed the ocean air for a living. But it was more than that; it was a passion. It was the life I knew.

Giana was the perfect distraction.

Her and that damn turtle.

"You're good to head out of here now, Declan," Gabriel said as he popped back into the room. I handed him the ice pack as I moved to place my feet on the floor. "I'll see you back here on Friday?"

I nodded and offered him a small smile. "I have no other plans, so I'll be here."

"I know you haven't been staying out of the water, but please refrain from surfing." There was a look of disapproval in his eyes, but he didn't dig in too deeply. "The last thing you need to do is mess your shoulder up even more and need surgery."

I raised an eyebrow at him as I rose to my feet and stepped toward the door. "How do you know I've been in the water?"

A chuckle escaped him as he shook his head. "Telling you to stay out of the water is like leading a dehydrated horse to water and telling them they can't drink."

"I'm not sure that's how that analogy goes."

He rolled his eyes. "You know exactly what I'm saying. Your brother told me."

Of course he did. Adrian couldn't keep anything to himself. Adrian was a sports medicine doctor who just so happened to be best friends with Gabriel. They both worked for the Orchid City Vipers—our city's professional hockey team—before Gabe started his own physical therapy practice.

"Yeah, well, Adrian needs to mind his own business."

Gabriel shrugged. "That's what happens when you're a professional athlete who has a brother who works in sports medicine. If anything, you should consider yourself lucky."

"You're probably right," I agreed with a shrug. "I'll see you Friday."

I left the office and headed out to my Jeep while simultaneously sending my brother a text. He was almost worse than my mother. She had been calling me incessantly since my injury. Thankfully, she didn't follow me here from California. The last thing I needed was someone else watching my every move.

As I started the engine, my phone vibrated with my brother's quick response.

ADRIAN

Sorry, little bro. Someone has to look out for you since you can't seem to do it yourself.

A sigh escaped me and I didn't bother answering him as I tossed my phone onto the passenger seat. There were still moments when he acted like he had to take care of me even though I was highly capable of doing it myself. I knew he was coming from a place of caring and concern, but shit. I could make my own decisions.

And I wasn't stupid enough to fuck my shoulder up even more than it was already.

I pulled my car out of the parking lot and began my drive toward the beach. It was about a ten-minute drive to the Orchid City Marine Research & Rehabilitation Center. I could have easily called to check in on Pop-Tart, but that meant I would have had to talk to someone other than Giana. I only cared to hear about the turtle's progress from her and no one else.

The one thing I loved about this town was the fact that everywhere you drove, you could feel the ocean. It was all around, constantly tantalizing your senses. The saltiness entered my nostrils and I could feel it in my veins. I breathed the scent in deeply, feeling it on my skin as I pulled down the drive that led to the facility buildings.

This time, I parked in a parking spot like a civilized person. The sun was hot on my skin and the air was thick with humidity as I crossed the pavement to the front doors. They slid open from the motion sensors and I welcomed the cold air as it sent a chill down my spine. There was an unfamiliar face at the front desk as I stepped up to it.

"Hi!" The younger girl, who appeared to be eighteen at most, smiled at me. "What can I do for you?"

I glanced around. "I was wondering if Giana was here today. I came by to see her."

The girl looked at me for a moment and I didn't miss the look of suspicion that passed through her eyes.

"She is. She's actually in the lab right now. Who should I tell her is here to see her?"

"Declan," I told her. "I brought in a turtle the other day, in case she doesn't remember me."

"Oh! You're the one who brought in Pop-Tart, right?"

I nodded, a smile pulling on my lips. My curiosity was piqued now. Had Giana been talking about me? Or perhaps it was just mentioned that someone had brought the turtle in after finding it on the beach.

"Let me go grab her," she said before disappearing through one of the doors that led to the back section of the facility. I began to wander around the lobby, reading over the different diagrams they had with information on the animals they housed and helped here. There was information on the different tours they offered, but just as I picked up a pamphlet, I heard her call my name.

"Declan," the girl said when she was back at the desk again. "She said she'll be right out."

Just as she spoke the words, Giana walked through the door behind her. My breath caught in my throat at the sheer sight of her. She looked just as I remembered from the other day. She wore a tight-fitting t-shirt that had the name of the center across her chest. Her bright blue eyes shimmered like the sun hitting the surface of the ocean. They widened slightly as she realized it was me.

I smiled brightly at her as I began to close the distance between us. She signed something to the other girl and she nodded before disappearing. Giana walked around to meet me in the center of the lobby, pulling a small notepad and pen from the back pocket of her jeans.

"Hey," I said softly, as her eyes dropped down to my mouth. She smiled back in response. "You said to check back in a few days about Pop-Tart."

I watched her hand clutch the pen as she scribbled something on a piece of paper. Guilt rushed through me. I hated that I didn't understand sign language. There had to be an easier way for the two of us to communicate.

You could have called.

That was it. My phone. I stared at her for a moment as I reached into my front pocket and pulled it out. I quickly unlocked the screen and went to a new message and handed it to Giana. "What's your phone number?"

Her eyebrows scrunched together in confusion.

"We can text, rather than you having to write everything out."

There was a look of hesitation that passed through the shimmering hues of blue in her irises. She knew my idea was more practical and I was sure it wasn't the first time she used it as a means for communicating with someone. Maybe just not with a stranger, which I practically was to her.

She took my phone from me. Her fingers brushed

against mine and it felt like a shock of electricity zapped through me. She inhaled sharply. The sensation instantly spread up my forearm, searing my skin. My fingertips were instantly warmed from the feeling of hers and I felt her absence as soon as she pulled away from me.

I watched her carefully as she typed her number into it and handed it back to me. This time, her fingers didn't touch mine. Giana slid her notepad and pen back into one of her pockets before pulling her phone out from another. I typed out the first message and sent it to her so she had my number.

DECLAN

Hey, it's Declan.

She glanced up at me with a smile playing on her lips as she raised an eyebrow.

GIANA

Obviously.

A chuckle rumbled in my chest. My lips parted and my gaze dropped down to my phone as I texted her back. It was different, standing here having a conversation like this, but there was a strange sense of intimacy to it. It was almost as if I could sense her sarcasm and personality through her words while reading her facial expressions.

DECLAN

This is Giana, right?

She pursed her lips, her nostrils flaring as she rolled her eyes and bit back her grin. She shook her head at me. Her eyes narrowed slightly as she studied me.

GIANA

You could have called.

I stared at her as I typed the words back to her and hit Send.

DECLAN

But then I wouldn't have been able to talk to you. And I wouldn't have gotten your number.

I watched her expression change and a pink tint spread across her cheeks as she kept her eyes trained on the screen in front of her. Her body was rigid and her chest rose quickly. She quickly recovered after she blinked a few times. She looked up at me and typed her response.

GIANA

Don't save my number, Declan.

A smirk played on my lips and our gazes collided. I simply shook my head at her.

DECLAN

I make no promises, princess. I might need to check in on Pop-Tart more than you expect. Speaking of, how is she doing?

Giana stared at me for a moment, almost as if I had left her speechless. She quickly snapped out of it and a smile formed on her lips.

GIANA

Come with me and I'll show you.

CHAPTER FOUR
GIANA

What the hell are you doing, Giana?

W   I had no business taking Declan back to see Pop-Tart, but here I was, leading the way through the facility until we got to the room with the recovery pools. I truly didn't expect him to show up again. Sure, he had said he would check in on her, but I really didn't think he would. And maybe that was a way of protecting myself since I was already distracted by his golden-colored eyes and the way they probed mine.

We only had three turtles that were in the recovery area right now and each of them were being quarantined so they were spaced out. I led Declan to the farthest pool in the room and stopped just outside of it as I motioned to Pop-Tart, where she was resting along the bottom.

I turned to look at Declan, studying his side profile

as he was looking down at the turtle. He was perfectly sculpted, chiseled to perfection by the ocean gods. He was like a statue from Atlantis that was handcrafted, not a single piece out of place.

Tearing my eyes away from his face, I began to type out a message on my phone to explain her condition and what we were expecting.

GIANA

The surgery was a little more extensive than we had anticipated. They were able to remove all of the fishing wire and repair her flipper. It's just a waiting game now. As long as everything heals appropriately and there aren't any complications, we should be able to rerelease her in a few months.

Declan read over the message and looked over to me, smiling brightly before responding.

DECLAN

It's that simple? You just fix her and can send her back on her way?

I nodded.

GIANA

That's what the goal is. If we are able to rehabilitate them and safely release them back into the wild, that's what we do. They belong in their natural habitats. The ones we can't release are the ones that we ultimately send to sanctuaries or aquariums.

He lifted his gaze back to the pool for a moment. I watched him as he stared down at Pop-Tart with a tender look. It was interesting, seeing someone have a reaction like this to an animal. Someone who didn't work directly with them the way I did. I had learned not to develop an emotional attachment to them, but that didn't diminish the way I cared for them.

Seeing Declan struck a chord in my heart. A chord that I didn't need to have touched. He was different compared to your common person who may stumble upon an injured turtle. The ocean had woven itself within the fibers of his soul. Declan had the ocean in him and he appreciated it. He didn't take it for granted. He had nothing but respect for the sea and the animals that inhabited it.

DECLAN

> I'm glad to hear that Pop-Tart's story should have a happy ending. She belongs in the ocean and I'm happy she will hopefully be returned there.

He turned to face me, his lips soft with the smile he had. He was unlike anyone I had ever met before. There was a tenderness, a gentleness that radiated from him.

GIANA

> We have no one to thank but you. If you hadn't found her when you did, she could have suffered a terrible fate.

He tilted his head to the side and his eyes slowly

explored mine. There was no urgency, but I couldn't quite figure out what he was searching for.

DECLAN

> She's lucky to have you taking care of her.

I couldn't help the warmth as it crept up my neck and spread across my cheeks. It was hard to not take his words like he was fishing for something more than just paying me a compliment. I didn't know what the intentions were behind his kind words, but a part of me couldn't help but wonder if that was all they really were.

Not everyone had an ulterior motive. Not everyone's actions and words were sprouting from a hidden agenda.

GIANA

> Would you like to see the rest of the facility?

I didn't know what had come over me to make the suggestion, but I needed to change the conversation. Declan Parks was practically a stranger. Just because we had a connection over the turtle he brought to the facility didn't mean there was any other kind of connection between us. He was genuinely interested in her recovery and nothing more.

DECLAN

I would love to.

Declan fell into step beside me as I took him on his own personal tour through the facility. We went through the different buildings and I explained the different areas and what was happening with the animals that were housed there. It was refreshing, being able to walk someone through with them actually being curious about it all.

Even though there was still a slight communication barrier between us, he hung on to every word I sent to him through our texting conversation. The phone proved to be very helpful, as it usually was. It was tiresome having to handwrite everything out to people. Declan was so immersed in learning everything he could about our mission and the animals.

We finished our tour and settled into a comfortable silence as we stepped out into the stuffy Florida air. There were some people the silence felt awkward with, but it was different with Declan. It was as if he was completely at ease with it, just walking beside me without having to fill the air with some type of conversation.

He respected the fact that I wasn't physically able to hear him speak. And instead of trying to force anything, he was just there. If there was one thing I learned about him in the short amount of time I knew him, it was that

Declan Parks was the type of authentic person who was content with just being.

There was nothing forced about him. He was taking life as it came, coasting through like he was riding the smoothest wave.

We rounded the front of the main building and he walked with me toward the entrance. There was no reason for him to come back inside, yet his steps didn't falter. He stayed right beside me.

DECLAN

What you guys are doing here is truly amazing. It's people like you who can save our planet.

I read over his words four times before I looked up at him. He was staring down at me with a mixture of emotion washing through his irises. I hadn't noticed the difference in our height until that moment. He was at least a foot taller than my five-foot-two stature and I had to tilt my head back a fraction to meet his gaze.

"You saved a turtle that was harmed from someone throwing trash into the ocean," he spoke the words aloud and my eyes were glued to his lips. *His perfectly plump lips.* It was the first time in my life I yearned to hear the sounds that flowed from them. "People are destroying our oceans and its natural inhabitants and you're out here fighting the fight, trying to save them."

His words resonated deep within my soul. Growing up alongside the ocean, I've watched the way humans have been slowly destroying it, along with the rest of our planet. I didn't go into marine biology to save the ocean, but instead to help do what I could to lessen the damage that was being done. There was so much harm done across every body of water and plain of land on earth.

GIANA

Without our oceans, we have nothing. I may not be able to save them all, but if I can save a few lives that our kind hurts in the process, then what I'm doing is worth it.

Hues of golden brown swirled in his irises as he read my message and looked back to me. "What do you study, specifically? It seems like you do a lot here in the facility."

His interest... it caught me off guard. When I told people I was a marine biologist, they never cared to ask about what I actually did. They just smiled and nodded, like it was a juvenile job. But Declan genuinely wanted to know.

GIANA

I study the disease processes caused in marine life from human pollution. And then I help out wherever I can in the facility, whether it's administering medications, helping with transports. Pretty much anything I can do to help.

He studied me with such curiosity. A smile played

on his lips and he shook his head at me. "How can you be so humble, doing what you do? You are literally the last hope we have. If only others cared as much as you do."

I scoffed.

GIANA

> I wouldn't have a job if people actually gave a shit about the environment.

Declan grinned, revealing his bright white teeth. His eyes shimmered under the light of the sun and they were pools of gold. Pools I could easily drown in and never resurface from.

"What can I do to help?"

His question took me by surprise. It was another question no one ever cared to ask.

GIANA

> Do you litter?

His eyebrows pulled together and he shook his head. "Absolutely not."

I mulled over his question, realizing I didn't have the perfect answer. It wasn't a problem that he could just solve. It was something that required spreading awareness to the masses. It had to be a collective effort and it was something that would never happen.

GIANA

I don't know if there's really anything that can be done. At least you're not contributing to the problem.

"There has to be something I can do." He paused for a moment and my eyes rested on his mouth. "Is there anything I can do to help you guys here? To help with what you're doing?"

I tilted my head to the side. He was a professional surfer who didn't even belong on this coast. Of course I looked up his social media accounts—*judge me.* It left me partially perplexed as to why he would want to volunteer his time here, but we did need all the help we could get.

GIANA

We can always use volunteers. I will have to talk to my boss and ask him about it.

"Perfect," he said with another smile that made my stomach do a somersault. "I want to know what happens with Pop-Tart, so I would love to help with the process or whatever you guys need help with. In the meantime, keep my phone number so you can let me know what he says."

My eyes widened and I began to shake my head. My heart thumped erratically in my chest to its own jagged beat.

"I told you I would not be making any promises

about what I did with your number, princess." He paused and showed his phone to me. "You're already saved in mine."

Why would you save my number?

Declan was already backing away from me with a playful grin. "You never know. I might find another injured turtle and need your assistance." He shrugged with indifference with a mischievous look in his golden eyes. "Or maybe I want to be able to talk to you whenever I'd like."

My heart felt like it was going to pound directly out of my chest. My stomach was doing its own gymnastics routine and it felt like my entire body was betraying me as warmth flooded my system.

"I'll talk to you soon, Giana," he said with a wink, still facing me so I could read his lips. "Enjoy the rest of your day," he said while walking backward.

He spun on his heel and walked to his car. I was frozen in place as I watched him climb into a black Jeep. He backed it out of the space he was in and threw up his hand to wave to me before he began to drive away. I stared after him, feeling completely at a loss for a single coherent thought.

Who knew all it would take was an injured turtle and a professional surfer to turn my life upside down?

CHAPTER FIVE
DECLAN

I slowly sipped my beer, watching golf on the TV at the bar. My brother, Adrian, sat next to me in silence as he lifted his own bottle to his lips and took a swig. Sounds of the ocean mixed with the voices of patrons traveled throughout the small bar. It was a pretty sweet place, situated at the end of one of the piers.

Adrian insisted on coming here and I was fairly certain he had something going on with one of the bartenders, but I wasn't going to question him on it. Pier Six seemed to be his place of choice when he wanted to go out, and I wasn't complaining. The atmosphere was exactly what I was looking for. Laid-back, go-with-the-flow vibes.

"So, how is physical therapy going?"

I raised a suspicious eyebrow at my brother. "I know you told Gabe I've been going out in the mornings."

He turned his head. "Because I've known you your entire life, Dec. You've always been shit at following directions."

"Well, I haven't been surfing. Just sitting out on my board."

Adrian shrugged. "Ultimately, it's your choice. I just figured Gabriel should know and chances are you weren't going to tell him."

I lifted my beer to my lips and the cold liquid slid down my throat as I took a long swallow. I set it down and looked back at my brother. "I've been careful. You don't have to worry about me."

Adrian snorted and shook his head. "I love your carefree attitude, but sometimes I feel like I need to smack some sense into you. If you were being careful, you wouldn't be floating in the ocean and rescuing turtles with a fucked-up shoulder."

"What was I supposed to do? Leave the turtle there?"

His chest rose and fell as he let out an exasperated sigh. "You could have called for someone to come pick it up like a normal person."

I cocked an eyebrow. "Does that sound like your brother?"

A soft laugh escaped him. "Absolutely not."

"Where's your favorite bartender tonight?" I asked him as the guy behind the bar tonight brought the food over that we ordered. "I didn't see her here."

Adrian pursed his lips and shrugged. "No idea what you're talking about."

My head tipped back and laughter spilled from my lips. "Come on, man. You've brought me here three different times and two of the times, I barely got in a word with you because you were too busy flirting with her."

He shook his head at me. "It's not like that at all. I just like coming here and we just so happen to get along."

"Yeah, okay," I snorted, shaking my head. "You tell yourself whatever you need to sleep at night."

Adrian gave me a dirty look and a sly smile as he ordered another round of beers along with shots. We both dug into our food and continued to drink well into the evening. I didn't bring up his love interest again, but I couldn't fight my mind as it kept drifting back to Giana. Something about the sea and the smell of the salt had her flooding my mind.

I couldn't explain it. It was almost as if the thought of her was tied to the one thing that ran through my veins. *The ocean air.*

"Okay, so I need to have a moment of truth with you," I said to Adrian as our plates were cleared away and the fifth round of beers wound up in front of us.

"Here we go." Adrian stared at me for a moment. "Do I even want to know?"

I scowled. "Why do you say it like that? It's not like it's something bad."

"I never know what the hell you're going to tell me." He let out a laugh. "Seriously, Dec. The last time you started a conversation with that, you told me you were going to Brazil for a year to live in a damn shack."

"Okay, first of all, that year was fucking amazing. Second of all, it wasn't a shack. It was a sweet little cottage that you enjoyed when you came to visit."

"It was like I couldn't reach the outside world with the limited cell service and no Wi-Fi," he said matter-of-factly.

I shrugged. "I would highly recommend unplugging like that to anyone who needs it. It's refreshing."

"The only thing refreshing about it was the fresh fruit, maybe."

I smiled at my too-civilized, too-reliant-on-technology brother. "See, I knew there were some things you liked about it."

"Your moment of truth," he waved his hand, motioning for me to continue. "Let's hear it."

I sucked in a breath. I had forgotten what even started our conversation, but was quickly reminded that it was me. Me and my damn thoughts of her. If it weren't for the alcohol and bonding moment, I would have kept it to myself. I had to tell someone about her.

"So, I met this girl and for the first time in my life, I don't know what to do."

Adrian's eyes widened and he cocked his head. "What do you mean? Why would you not know what to do?"

"I don't know, man." I ran a frustrated hand through my hair as I took another swig of my beer. "She's a marine biologist at the place where I dropped off that turtle."

"That explains why you went back there again."

"Well, no," I argued and shook my head. "I wanted to check in on the turtle too."

Adrian gave me a pointed look and rolled his eyes. "Sure. So, what is the problem then?"

"Is it too soon to go back and check in again?"

He fought back a smile and choked back a laugh. "Yes. You just went there, don't go back again."

"Dude, I know." I shook my head, feeling the alcohol entangling its warmth in my brain. "I don't want her to think I'm psychotic or anything, but I want to see her."

"I thought you were going there for the turtle?"

I narrowed my eyes at him as he smirked at me. "Goddammit."

"At least give it a few days, Dec. You don't want to come on too strong."

I nodded, agreeing with him. "That's what I was thinking. You know how I live my life. It's weird having someone stuck in my head like this."

"Oh, I know," Adrian agreed with a chuckle. "I feel like the last time I saw you worked up over a girl was back in high school when Melanie Dean refused to go to prom with you."

"That whole thing was fucked up," I scoffed. "She

wanted everyone to think we were together and then went with Patterson Yangley instead."

Adrian was still laughing and shaking his head. "I remember it clearly." He pushed away from the bar and rose to his feet. "I'm going to head to the bathroom. Ask Bentley for our bill and then we can head out."

I nodded as he disappeared and drained the rest of my beer from the glass bottle before setting it down. Bentley was helping someone else at the moment, so I pulled out my phone to check the time. My mind didn't even register it as I began to scroll through the different apps, ultimately ending up on my messages.

Opening the thread between Giana and me from yesterday, I couldn't help but smile as I read back over the messages. The last one was her asking me why I would save her number. The memory played over in my mind and my response. I couldn't stop myself as my fingers began to move across the screen.

DECLAN

Hey you.

I stared at the message, instantly regretting it. I wasn't wasted, but I had a good buzz going and I didn't think through what I was saying to her properly. She surprised me as three bubbles popped up before my phone vibrated with her response.

GIANA

Hey yourself.

48

Okay. I could work with this. I wasn't exactly sure what I was doing here, but she was opening the door for conversation. She probably shouldn't have done that, not when I was feeling the way I was. The warmth spread through my body and part of it was from the alcohol, but it was also from the dopamine Giana's response was giving me.

GIANA

Did you happen to come across another injured turtle?

A smile was pulling on the corners of my lips and I didn't give a shit as I grinned like a fool. She remembered what I told her about saving her number.

DECLAN

Not today. I just decided I wanted to talk to you instead.

"What are you smiling about?" My brother's voice broke through my daze. I lifted my eyes up to his. "You didn't get the check, did you?"

"What?" I stared at him in confusion before remembering what he had asked of me. "Oh, no. I forgot."

Adrian shook his head at me as my phone vibrated and I directed my attention back to my messages as he called for Bentley and paid for our tab.

GIANA

I was beginning to wonder if you were being serious or not about that.

DECLAN

> As serious as a fucking shark attack, princess.

> I want to be able to talk to you whenever I want... unless that's not what you want.

I locked my screen and held my phone in my hand as I rose to my feet. Adrian was waiting for me and I followed him down the pier, making our way toward the beach. My phone vibrated again and I slowed my footsteps as I looked at it.

GIANA

> If I didn't want you to have my number, I never would have given it to you.

I smiled down at my phone as I read over her message twice. My vision was a little fuzzy and the words kind of blurred together.

"Come on, lover boy," my brother called to me from where he was already standing at the end of the pier. "You can talk to her when we get home."

It was only a five-minute walk back to Adrian's house and my legs felt like they had sandbags weighing them down. I was exhausted from the day and drinking hadn't helped to chase that away. My heart beat a little harder in my chest as my phone burned a hole in my pocket.

Adrian slipped into his room and I dropped down on the couch as soon as I walked inside. I rolled onto my side, settling into the cushions, still dressed in the clothes I wore all day. I knew I needed to get up but my eyelids were growing heavier with every passing second. Fishing out my phone from my pocket, I typed out another message to Giana.

DECLAN

Can I come see you and Pop-Tart soon?

I could barely keep my eyes open as sleep was quickly taking over me. My phone vibrated once more and I read her message, a smile pulling on my lips as I let sleep pull me under. It was blue like the ocean. Just like her eyes.

GIANA

You know where to find us.

CHAPTER SIX
GIANA

I didn't hear from Declan after the other night. It surprised me when his name came across my phone with a message. He wasn't specific on when he was going to stop by the rehab center again, but it was now Saturday. I was off for the weekend and our weekend crew would be tending to the animals. My schedule was only Monday through Friday, unless they absolutely needed me there.

It was early in the morning and I went out to the beach to watch the sunrise. With work, I wasn't always able to get out here, but it was something I liked to do when I had the chance. I loved this time of the day. I lived in silence already, but there was something enchanting about early mornings.

I was habitually an early riser and I enjoyed the walk to the ocean. The feeling of the sand between my toes was nostalgic. It made me think of my mother.

When my brother and I were little, she used to take us to watch the sunrise. We would watch the dolphins and bring shells home. But she always insisted that we walk barefoot.

She loved to dig her toes into the sand. She loved connecting with the earth and nature on an intimate level. She was the one who taught me to love and appreciate the world around us. She was the reason why I was doing the work I was doing.

I stared down at my pedicured feet as I buried my toes beneath the granules. My eyelids fluttered shut and I inhaled the smell of the salty air, envisioning my mother with me. Her soft blonde curls furling around her face from the breeze that drifted across the ocean.

She was so beautiful—inside and out. And damn, I missed her. I was thankful for my brother Nico and for how close we were, but it just wasn't the same. No one would ever come close to her, and I knew he missed her as deeply as I did.

Lifting my head, I opened my eyes and looked back out at the sea as the sun was cresting the horizon. "I wish you were here, Mom," I mouthed the words into the void. The light shimmered across the surface of the ocean.

Bending my knees, I lowered myself down to sit on the beach. I wasn't sure how long I sat there, watching the sun lift higher and higher into the sky. I was lost in my thoughts, in a world of my own that was encapsulated in silence. Fingers tapped softly on my shoulder, startling me as my entire body lifted from the ground.

I whipped my head around, my eyes wide with fear until they landed on his golden ones. "Declan?" I mouthed as an overwhelming sense of relief mixed with confusion that instantly flooded me.

He flashed me that damn smile, equipped with dimples and all as he dropped down onto the beach beside me. Droplets of water dripped onto his forehead from his wet, wavy hair. I resisted the urge to brush them away. I refused to let my eyes trail away from his face. He was only wearing board shorts and I knew I would be done for if I traced the curves and planes of his body with my gaze.

"Top of the morning to you." His lips moved with the words as he continued to smile at me. "What brings you out here this early?"

I lifted my hands and went to sign back to him, but remembered he wouldn't be able to understand me. His face fell, the smile sliding off his lips in an instant. His eyebrows pulled together and I watched his throat bob as he swallowed roughly. I pulled my phone from the front pocket of my hoodie and showed it to him with a reassuring smile.

His lips lifted but the smile didn't reach his eyes as he nodded.

I typed out a message before handing my phone to him. He wrapped his hand around mine and didn't take the device from me. His bare knee brushed against mine. Everywhere his skin touched me lit up my nerve endings.

GIANA

I like coming out here in the mornings when it's calm and quiet. It's peaceful and comforting.

His eyes were soft and warm. "You're an ocean soul too, aren't you?"

I nodded, typing something out as he held his hand over mine while I was holding the phone.

GIANA

I grew up with the ocean and it's the only life I've ever known. I've learned to respect her and appreciate the wonders and beauties she holds.

"She's pretty fucking magnificent, isn't she?" His lips moved and I watched them, completely captivated and mesmerized. "The beauty of the ocean doesn't come close to touching you, though."

The air left my lungs in a rush and I froze under his gaze. My stomach flipped and my heart pounded against my ribcage. I had to have been imagining it. I had to have read his lips incorrectly. My lips parted slightly and a shallow breath escaped me.

"Do you know how to surf?"

He was suddenly switching gears, but he was switching them effortlessly. The words he spoke were heavily laced within the salty air between us even though neither of us acknowledged them. The air between us crackled with electricity.

I shook my head and tapped my fingers on the screen of my phone again.

GIANA

We don't really have the waves for it here. I tried when I was younger, but never really knew how to do it properly.

"Maybe I can show you sometime."

I stared at him, counting five of my heartbeats. He was throwing me off guard. I felt like I was trapped within his waves, unsure of how to break through the surface.

GIANA

What are your intentions, Declan? I know you're not just talking to me because of Pop-Tart.

His eyes shimmered under the sun and I caught specks of green around his pupils. "You're right," he admitted with no hesitation. "I'm fully invested in Pop-Tart's recovery, but she isn't the only one who caught my attention. I want to know more about you, Giana. I want to know *you*."

His words caught me off guard and I was lost in the shifting golden hues of his irises. A million questions ran through my mind. Consider it fate that he walked into my life. It was as if the ocean gifted him to me by presenting him with an injured turtle. The way the dots connected, it sent a warmth flooding through my body.

"Time is fleeting, life is short. People come and go, and I don't form attachments." He said it with such simplicity, yet his eyes were burning directly through mine. "I don't often take an interest in people, but there's something about you. Something that makes me want to know what makes you tick. You have my attention and I can't shake it off."

It took my brain a moment to catch up as I processed everything he said. Over the years, I had learned how to read lips well, but there were times when my brain almost lagged. It was if everything needed a moment to sink in after I fully absorbed the words.

"You have my attention and I can't shake it off."

I swallowed roughly over the lump that formed in my throat. Besides my friends and family, it wasn't often that I had someone's undivided attention. I didn't let people get close enough that they would be able to hurt me. I knew I was treated differently by some because of my hearing deficit. I didn't fault them for it.

I just understood how some people worked.

And at the end of the day, you were always disposable in someone else's life.

There was something different about Declan, but I didn't repeat the words back to him. Something about him called to me. Like our souls had once known one another and they were reconnecting. We had so much in common. He was so attentive and interested in everything I told him. I couldn't quite explain it.

We were both ocean souls.

We breathed the same salty air. We both had the sea running rampant through our veins.

His hand was still closed over mine as I held on to my phone. My skin burned from his touch, setting forth an internal inferno. My fingers moved diligently and lightly as I tapped another message on the screen.

GIANA

What do you want to know?

I lifted my gaze to his. He was so close, I could smell the ocean on his skin. His hair had since grown damp and his eyes were glistening beneath the rays of light from the sun traveling through the sky. His lips parted. I dropped my eyes to them.

"Everything."

CHAPTER SEVEN
DECLAN

The sun was already climbing higher into the sky and I stared at Giana, lost in her bright blue eyes as we sat on the beach. I could sit here and watch her all goddamn day. Her eyes bounced between mine. I wasn't lying. I wanted to know everything I possibly could about her.

Freckles were sprinkled across the bridge of her nose, spilling across her cheeks. I wanted to memorize every single one. My eyes traveled across her perfectly symmetrical features. There wasn't a single imperfection and even if there were, she still would have been perfect in my eyes. There was a small scar just below her eyebrow. I fought the urge to reach out and touch it.

"Are you hungry?"

She tilted her head to the side, her eyebrows pulling together. My swift movements through conversation were throwing her off-balance and I instantly felt a twinge of guilt.

"Come get breakfast with me?" I offered, my voice quiet. I was always relatively confident and it was rare that I questioned my own words or thoughts. Giana had me questioning everything. I just wanted it to be right. Everything needed to be right for her.

She studied me for a moment, her expression softening. I watched her gaze as she directed it out to the ocean and she stared out into the distance. My breath was frozen within my lungs and I waited. Finally she looked back at me, a small smile on her plump lips as she nodded.

I sighed a breath of relief. For a second, I was afraid she was going to turn me down. I climbed to my feet and held out my hand for her. Her chest rose and fell as she stared at my hand for a fraction of a second before sliding hers into mine. Her skin was warm against mine and I helped her to her feet before releasing her.

Giana took a moment to brush the sand away from her body. My shorts were mostly dry. She bent down to grab her flip-flops and we walked side by side until we reached the end of the beach. The sand was like powder, so we bypassed the showers that were off to the side. Giana walked ahead of me, but as we reached the street, my hand darted out to grab her wrist.

She turned back to look at me with surprise laced within her expression.

"I need to get a shirt from my car," I explained to

her, motioning over to where my Jeep was. I had a clean t-shirt I threw in there this morning. I let go of her wrist and she waited for me as I jogged over and grabbed my shirt.

When I returned, Giana had her phone out with a message already typed out for me.

GIANA

Where did you want to go to eat?

"Have you ever been to Rads by the Sea? They have a great breakfast menu."

She nodded, erased her message, and typed a new one before handing the phone back to me. Our fingers brushed against one another's and I felt the spark of electricity run up my forearms.

GIANA

I've been there before, but only for dinner.

"Well, allow me to introduce you to their amazing breakfast options."

She smiled brightly and her shoulders shook as she laughed silently. My ears craved to hear something from her, but it was something I would never ask of her. I wanted to know whatever Giana wanted me to know. I would never ask her anything that would be too invasive unless she opened the door for that.

She motioned for us to walk down the street and I easily fell into step beside her.

I was following her lead. I would go wherever the tides between us decided to take us.

It was a short walk, only about three minutes, before we were standing out in front of the restaurant. It was situated just along the beach. It was built up on a hill and the seating area was on the second floor which allowed you to look out over the ocean. It was one of my favorite places to come to when I was in Orchid City.

The silence between us was comfortable. She paused for a moment and I pulled the door open for her, allowing her to go in before me. I followed after her as she began to climb the stairs in front of us. We reached the second floor and stepped up to the hostess desk where a young man greeted the two of us.

Giana smiled and glanced to me with a nervous look in her eyes. She never once reached for a notepad while we were on the beach. She was wearing a hooded sweatshirt and a pair of black cotton shorts. The only thing she had with her was her phone.

"Just the two of you?" the guy said as he grabbed two menus.

I nodded. "Can we sit outside? Somewhere where we can see the ocean."

"Absolutely," he confirmed and began to lead the way.

I caught Giana's eye once more. "Don't worry about it. I got you."

I didn't miss the wave of relief that washed through

her eyes and the way her body visibly relaxed. It struck a nerve inside of me. Guilt flooded me in an instant. I had thought about our communication barrier and how we worked around it, but I never once considered how hard day-to-day life must have been for her.

Most people weren't familiar with sign language. It must have been difficult trying to communicate with people around her, conforming to means of speaking that they understood, rather than the other way around. How many people went out of their way to accommodate Giana?

We were seated at a table that had a perfect view of the ocean. I followed Giana's gaze out to the sea, watching a pod of dolphins popping out of the water every so often. I couldn't stop my eyes as they trailed back to her face, and I watched her as she watched them. A soft smile pulled on the corners of her lips and her eyes squinted ever so slightly.

I leaned forward, my hand touching her forearm as I got her attention. Giana looked back to me, the same smile still on her lips.

"What do you want to drink? I can order when they come over."

She nodded and pulled out her phone before typing something on it. She set it down on the table and slid it over to me. I picked it up and read the message.

GIANA

I'll have whatever you're having.

I looked up and smiled at her, just as our server walked over to the table. She looked between the two of us, introducing herself and asking if we wanted to place our drink orders. Neither of us had looked at the menu, so I ordered each of us a glass of water and mimosas. I didn't miss the way Giana raised an eyebrow, but she didn't question me on it.

I slid the phone back to her. "Tell me your story."

Her eyes were trained on mine, studying me for a beat. A sigh escaped her and she picked up the phone, as she began to type it out. Her sigh didn't appear to be from annoyance, but it pained me nonetheless. I instantly felt like shit for asking her to do so. My dumb ass didn't take into consideration that she was going to literally have to type out every single word.

Much to my dismay, when she finally slid her phone back to me, there was only one simple sentence.

GIANA

I don't have a story to tell.

My lips pursed. I refused to accept that. I looked back up at her, just as our server appeared with our drinks. She asked if we were ready to order. I looked to Giana and she shook her head.

"I'll give the two of you a few more minutes to look over the menu," our server replied with a smile before disappearing once again.

My eyes met Giana's. "I refuse to believe you have nothing to tell. Figure out what you want to eat." She attempted to reach for the phone, but I pulled it away and shook my head. "No arguing, princess."

She cut her eyes at me and it lit a spark inside of me. I knew there was more to her than the peaceful, happy persona she projected to everyone. There was a fire burning inside of her and I wanted to see her flames.

Giana picked out a fresh fruit crepe and pointed it out to me on the menu. Our server came back to the table shortly after and I ordered a breakfast sandwich for myself before telling her what Giana wanted.

"I'm so sorry. We actually ran out of strawberries this morning," she said with a frown. "Would raspberries be okay to substitute with?"

I looked over at Giana, who was staring out at the ocean again. She was completely oblivious, not necessarily by choice. I reached out and touched her forearm again, gaining her attention. She whipped her head to look at me, her eyes slightly panicked as she looked at me and the woman standing by the table.

"They're out of strawberries. Are raspberries okay instead?"

Her throat bobbed as she swallowed roughly and nodded. She forced a smile on her face and looked at the woman and nodded at her too. I didn't miss the look of confusion and curiosity on our server's face as she wrote down our order and left the two of us alone.

I stared at Giana, watching her as she pulled her silverware from the napkin in front of her. She positioned them one by one before laying the napkin across her lap. I wanted inside her head. I wanted to read her damn thoughts. She looked back up at me.

"Does that happen a lot?"

She raised a questioning eyebrow for me to elaborate.

"Communicating with people. Is it always like that?"

She frowned, nodded, and grabbed her phone. I watched her expression, her eyebrows pinched tightly together as she furiously typed something out and handed the phone back to me.

GIANA

It's been like that since I lost my hearing as a child. It's easier for me because I can read lips, but there aren't many people I encounter who are able to do the same or who know sign language. My notepad and pen help. I didn't bring them with me this morning.

I wasn't expecting that. Well, the communication part, I was. Not about her losing her hearing as a child. That was slightly unexpected.

"What happened?" I paused for a moment. "If you don't want to talk about it, I understand."

Her lips twitched and she motioned for me to hand her the phone, to which I did. I enjoyed watching the way her face transformed while she was typing and deleting and retyping her message. She was so expressive without even realizing it. It was amazing, in all honesty. Her sense of hearing had diminished, but her nonverbal communication was compensating for her loss.

GIANA

> I was eight years old when it happened. I was incredibly sick from the flu and it was damaging my heart. My body responded to the medications they put me on to protect my heart and fix the damage, but I ended up having a bad reaction that caused permanent profound hearing loss.

I read her message once, twice, three times as the words sank in. My heart broke for her as the reality hit me in the chest like a ton of bricks. The thought of her once being able to hear and then having it ripped away from her so abruptly. I couldn't even imagine.

In that moment, I knew exactly what I needed to do. I wanted to make things easier in her life, not harder. I needed to learn how to communicate with her, the way she knew how to. I was going to learn ASL.

"I'm sorry that happened to you," I told her softly. "That must have been frightening."

She shrugged and offered a sad smile as she picked up the phone and typed something else out.

GIANA

> It was, but that was a long time ago now. I honestly don't really remember what it was like, except I still can hear in my dreams, so that's always comforting. Now, tell me something about you.

A smile tugged on my lips. A chuckle vibrated in my chest as she pulled a page from my own book. I liked it. The sudden shift in conversation. She kept me on my toes.

"There's not much to tell," I replied with a wink before taking a sip of my mimosa.

Giana narrowed her eyes at me and pursed her lips in defiance and disbelief.

"I have a specific pair of board shorts that I have to wear for every competition I surf in."

She lifted the phone from the table and her fingers moved across the screen.

GIANA

> Does that actually work?

I thought of my shoulder and frowned. "Well, it did. Until it didn't anymore." I met her gaze that was filled with curiosity. "I dislocated my shoulder a few weeks ago at a competition in Hawaii. I came here to stay with my brother while I'm going through physical therapy."

Her eyes jumped back and forth between both of my shoulders.

"My left one."

Her eyes met mine with a ghost of a smile written across her lips.

GIANA

Just like Pop-Tart's...

It's almost as if it were fate.

My breath caught in my throat and I swallowed roughly. "And this?" I questioned her. "Is this fate too?"

She winked as she showed her phone to me once more.

GIANA

Maybe it is... or maybe it's just breakfast.

CHAPTER EIGHT

GIANA

Rolling over in bed, I looked at my phone to check the time. I hadn't set an alarm to watch the sunrise and when I saw it was already quarter past nine, I was far too late to catch a piece of it now. My room was dark as I closed my curtains before climbing back into bed, so I could to enjoy my morning of peace. I didn't have any plans for today, there was nowhere I needed to be. Staying in bed a little while longer seemed like the perfect start to a lazy Sunday.

Nestling my head deeper into the pillow, I closed my eyes and pulled the blankets back up to my chin. My eyelids fluttered shut and it didn't take long before sleep began to creep in. I was somewhere between being half awake and slipping into the darkness when a harsh light was abruptly cast across my room. I could see it with my eyes closed.

I opened them, quickly sitting up as I saw someone viciously pulling open my curtains. My heart raced in my chest and I was in a state of fright while my eyes adjusted to the light. Instantly, relief swept through me and I narrowed my eyes at my brother's back.

He turned around, smiling brightly as his blue eyes met mine. "Rise and shine," he spoke the words while simultaneously signing them to me.

I gave him the middle finger before signing back to him. *"Go away, Nico."*

He shook his head. "Nope. Come on. Out of bed," he urged as he walked over and pulled the blankets away from me. "Wes and I brought breakfast."

"I'm not hungry."

My stomach betrayed me as it growled. Nico rolled his eyes. "Quit being dramatic." He spun on his heel without another word and marched out of my bedroom.

An exaggerated sigh escaped me. I climbed out of bed, even though I just wanted to stay there for a little while longer. I knew my brother and his persistence. If I didn't come out, he'd come back in for me.

I slid my feet into my slippers and adjusted my pajama shorts before making my way out into the kitchen. Wes was sitting at the breakfast bar with his back to me and Nico was opposite of him, pulling Styrofoam containers out of a plastic bag.

Weston Cole was my brother's best friend. He was

an interesting character who was the peanut butter to Nico's jelly. My brother was a little more on the serious side whereas Wes was constantly cracking jokes. He had a way of keeping things lighthearted, but I knew there was more to him beneath the surface.

One night when he was drunk, he had admitted to me that he essentially grew up caring for his little brother. His father was never in the picture and his mother had lost her parental rights when he was ten. He grew up living with his grandparents, but he was the one who was always looking out for his little brother.

He never gave me any more than that, but he had his own struggles he didn't like to talk about. He masked everything with a smile and a joke.

Nico lifted his head as he handed Wes his food. A smile worked its way onto his lips and there was a look of satisfaction as he saw me walking into the kitchen. Wes turned halfway, looking over his shoulder at me with a grin.

"Hey, G," he nodded at me and motioned for me to sit down next to him. "Aren't you usually awake by now?"

I shrugged. *"I forgot to set my alarm so I figured I would enjoy being able to sleep in… until the two of you rudely interrupted."*

I sat down and Nico placed a container in front of me. I popped it open and smiled at a heaping pile of pancakes with fruit. My stomach growled yet again in betrayal.

"Thought you said you weren't hungry?" Nico questioned me with an eyebrow raised.

I gave him the middle finger again before smothering my food in maple syrup. Wes had already turned his attention back to his own breakfast. My brother was staring at me with a suspicious look on his face as he shoveled a mouthful of eggs between his lips.

Sliding my knife through the pancakes, I cut them into pieces before I realized he was looking at me. My eyebrows were pinched together as I stared back at him. *"What?"* I mouthed to him before taking a bite of my pancakes.

"Wes and I stopped by yesterday morning with food, but you never came back."

"Since when do the two of you show up with random meals?" I asked him with my hands. *"Do you frequently abandon your girlfriend to have breakfast with your boyfriend?"*

"As much as I love your brother, it's strictly platonic," Wes spoke after reading my signs. "He's not my type anyways. I prefer blondes."

I rolled my eyes at him. I was always grateful when someone took the time to learn ASL so they could communicate with me, but there were times I wished they didn't. Right now was one of those times because I didn't need Wes's commentary, even though it did make me involuntarily smile.

"Harper had a pregnancy announcement shoot yesterday morning and she's prepping for a wedding today," Nico informed me. "Wes just so happens to not have any other friends, so he's my second choice to her."

"Hey. I will never be someone's second choice." Wes gave Nico a disapproving look, although there was a playfulness to it.

"Looks like you already are," I signed to him while rolling my eyes. I turned my attention back to my brother. *"I ended up getting breakfast with a friend."*

His forehead creased. "I thought Winter and Kai were out of the country?"

Shit.

It was none of his business, but like I had already mentioned before, my brother was persistent as hell and he made it his life's mission to keep a watchful eye on me. Even as a grown adult, he still felt it was his duty to make sure I was safe. I appreciated it always, but there were times he was borderline overbearing.

"She is... I went with another friend."

I didn't know if Declan was necessarily my friend, but that was what we were going with.

"Who's the friend?" Wes questioned me after swallowing a mouthful of food.

I hesitated for a moment and abruptly got up from my seat to fetch a glass of orange juice. The two of them were waiting for a response. I wasn't sure if I should tell them his real name or make something up. Who knew where things were even going between the two of us, if they were going anywhere.

When I walked back over to my seat, I saw the screen of my phone lit up on the counter and Wes was looking at it like the nosy bastard he was. I quickly snatched it away and flipped it upside down on the other side of my container of food.

"Who's Declan?" he asked me.

My brother tilted his head to the side. "That's a new name. Is that your new friend?"

Dammit.

I took a sip of my orange juice, swallowing roughly as I nodded. *"I met him a week or so ago when he brought in an injured turtle. We ran into one another at the beach yesterday morning and he invited me to breakfast."*

"A breakfast date?" Wes asked, speaking at the exact time Nico did.

"Declan who?"

"I doubt you know him. He's not from around here."

Nico pursed his lips. "That doesn't mean shit. If someone is taking my sister on fucking breakfast dates, I want to know who he is."

I ran a frustrated hand down my face. *"His name is Declan Parks. He's just here visiting his brother while he rehabs his shoulder that he injured surfing."*

Wes's face lit up. "Declan Parks. Like the best surfer in the country?"

I shrugged. I knew he was a professional surfer, but it wasn't like I followed the sport. *"I guess?"*

"I don't give two shits who he is or what he does. If he's taking my sister on dates, I want to meet him." His nostrils flared and he shook his head. "I've never taken a girl to breakfast before besides Harper."

Wes nodded. "Yeah. Dinner is cool because you usually end up following up with dessert later on. Breakfast feels too... intimate or something."

Nico gave Wes a murderous glare before looking back at me.

"It wasn't a date. And I told you—he's just a friend, kind of."

"Kind of?" Nico retorted. "If he's not a friend, then what is he?"

"I meant kind of because I barely even know the guy." I let out an exasperated sigh as I shook my head at him. *"It was seriously nothing."*

"Was it, though, if he's texting you?" Wes chimed in, and I fought the urge to drive my fist into the side of his face. He was not helping the matter. "What did he say to you anyways?"

I rolled my eyes at the two of them and unlocked my phone before opening up the unread message. My stomach felt like it was already on the floor and my heart was drumming away in my chest. I couldn't help the butterfly feelings I had.

DECLAN

Good morning, princess. I missed you at sunrise.

Oh my god. My heart skipped a beat. We never agreed on meeting again this morning, but he noticed my absence regardless. I quickly typed back a response to him, fighting a smile.

GIANA

> I forgot to set an alarm and overslept. My brother and his friend are here right now asking about you.

"He was just saying good morning."

Nico's face scrunched, like he didn't believe me, but the two of them didn't press any further as they both directed their attention back to their food. Wes asked Nico something about hockey and I took that as my out of the conversation. My phone vibrated from where I set it on my lap and I opened up the message.

DECLAN

> So, you've been talking about me then?

I pulled my lips between my teeth as the butterflies in my stomach fluttered their wings.

GIANA

> I may have mentioned you.

I was fully ignoring my brother and his friend as I continued to eat and text Declan.

DECLAN

> I hope you put in a good word for me because I'd like to see you again.

> I did, but he prefers to form his own opinions of people.

Nico tapped on the counter to get my attention. I lifted my gaze to his with a stupid grin on my face. "If you're going to be hanging out with him, I want to make sure he's not a piece of shit, G."

"I appreciate your concern, but I don't need you scaring him away."

He let out a breath. "Fine, but if things get more serious, I'm going to need to meet him."

"Okay," I agreed with a nod. "I will keep that in mind."

My phone vibrated again and I looked down at Declan's message as it lit up the screen. There was no reason for Nico to meet him now. After all, it was just breakfast, right? There was no way this could possibly go any further than that, even if I did find myself drawn to him.

DECLAN

> He's protective of you, as he should be. I don't mean to be forward, but I have every intention of getting to know you, Giana. If your brother wants to meet me, I will gladly do that.

My breath caught in my throat. My experience with other men had been limited. In a way, this was foreign territory to me. It felt like things were shifting quickly, but I wasn't afraid of it. I wasn't upset with it. Instead, I was having the opposite reaction.

I was ready to dive in deep.

CHAPTER NINE
DECLAN

I stared at my laptop screen, moving my hands along as I spoke the words aloud. The instructor who was on the opposite end of the Zoom call moved his along with me. He was going through basic questions to start a conversation. I was fairly certain I was fucking it all up, but I felt like I was slowly getting the hang of it too.

This was only my second session with Mark. I found him online two days ago and signed up for an hour of ASL lessons with him every day. The first day he taught me the alphabet and a few common signs. He sent along a PDF that had visuals of the signs and I practiced them every spare second I had in the day.

"You're learning really quickly, Declan," Mark said with a smile as we wrapped up our lesson. My email dinged as he sent over the document of everything we had gone over today. "If you have the time to practice the signs you learned today, that would be perfect and we can expand on them tomorrow morning."

I folded my hands on the table on Adrian's back deck as I watched my screen. A part of me was happy with the progress I had made, but I felt like it wasn't enough. It wasn't something I could learn overnight. It took time, and I found myself struggling to have any ounce of patience.

"Is there any way I can learn faster?" The frustration was evident in my voice and it was laced throughout my words.

Mark let out a laugh. "I've never had someone pick up on it like you have. It's all about memorizing and muscle memory of how you move your arms, hands, and fingers." He paused for a moment as a look of curiosity passed through his expression. "May I ask what the rush is for?"

I sucked in a deep breath before letting it out. "I'd like to be able to communicate with a friend without her having to write it down or text it to me."

"Ah," he said with a knowing look. He understood completely, without me having to divulge any more details. "Well, regardless of your progress—which has been amazing—I'm sure she will just be thrilled to know you are taking an interest in learning ASL."

"I hope so," I said softly, praying to the ocean gods that he was right.

"Has she told you about sign names at all?" Mark questioned me.

I shook my head, my eyebrows pulling together. "What's a sign name?"

"It's like a special sign that someone gives someone instead of having to spell out their name every time."

I mulled over his words. "I did notice that when she says her brother's name, she does this thing where she signs the letter N by her forehead."

Mark nodded. "That would make a lot of sense, since he's her brother and if his name starts with the letter N."

"I don't think she has one for me."

Mark smiled. "Not yet."

His words swirled around in my brain and I couldn't help but think about the significance of a sign name. Maybe she did have one for me and I didn't know.

"Tomorrow at eight again?"

Mark nodded. "I will see you then."

We both ended the Zoom call and my screen went momentarily black. There was movement from behind me. I saw the reflection of my brother standing off to the side, hovering in the doorway. Turning around in my seat, I glanced at him, feeling like I had just been caught doing something I wasn't supposed to be doing.

He stepped out onto the deck in silence as he walked over to where I was sitting and took a seat across from me at the table. "What was that about?" He had a mug in one hand and a glass in the other. He had brought himself his morning coffee and a glass of orange juice for me. He knew me well enough to know I was never a coffee drinker.

I put my laptop in sleep mode and slowly shut it. I took the glass he was holding out to me and took a sip of the tangy liquid. Hesitation lingered, but I admitted what I was doing. "I'm taking sign language lessons."

A confused look washed over Adrian's face as he set his mug down in front of him. "For what, exactly?"

"So I can talk to Giana."

He raised his eyebrows at me with a devious look in his honey-colored irises. "Is that the girl with the turtle?"

I rolled my eyes at his words. "Yes."

My brother stared at me for a moment. It was as if he were studying me or lost in his own thoughts. His face instantly lit up with a touch of curiosity lingering in his expression. "Wait. What is her last name?"

"I don't know," I admitted, suddenly feeling guilty for not knowing it. Was that something I should have known by now? "I didn't ask her what it was and she didn't offer it up."

"I'm pretty sure I know her." He paused as he pulled out his phone. "Well, I know of her. We've only met a few times, if it's the Giana I think it is."

He handed me his phone which he had opened up to some hockey player's Instagram account. It was a picture of the guy sitting down with Giana leaning over his back. Her arms were wrapped around his neck and she was smiling brightly at whoever took the picture of them. I glanced at the Instagram handle. *Nico Cirone.* I hated him instantly.

I didn't even think to ask her if she was seeing anyone. I just fucking assumed like a dumbass. She never mentioned anyone, not that it ever came up in conversation. Although, if she had a boyfriend, she wouldn't have just gone along with some of the things I had said to her. I literally told her I wanted to know everything about her. That wasn't exactly something you said to someone you weren't interested in on a deeper level.

"Well, fuck," I muttered as I handed him his phone in defeat. I couldn't help but feel completely blindsided and stupid. "I didn't know she was seeing someone. Who is he? Does he play for the Vipers?"

My brother stared at me for a moment before he let out a loud laugh and smacked the back of my head. "That's her brother, you idiot. He plays for the Vipers. Giana has come with him to some of the different family functions."

My mouth instantly formed an O. I took his phone from him again and looked at the picture. The color of their hair was almost identical. Their eyes both shimmered blue like the ocean. Their bone structure even similar. I should have noticed it at first, but I was blinded by the thought of her having a boyfriend. It made sense now. They looked like they were brother and sister.

I let out a breath of relief, taking back the thought in

my head of hating him. He was a bit of a threat, considering how protective he seemed to be of his sister, but he wasn't a threat in the way I had first pictured him.

"So, she is single then?" I questioned Adrian as I held his phone out to him again.

He took it from me and shrugged. "That wasn't something you ever thought to maybe ask her before you decided to become obsessed with her and take ASL lessons?"

I choked out a laugh. "Nope. The thought never honestly crossed my mind."

"Sometimes I wonder about you," Adrian mused out loud, his mouth twitching. "Have you taken too many spills into the dangerous waves while surfing? Or maybe all the salt water you've been living in has begun to dry out your brain."

"Fuck you," I mumbled as I attempted to keep a straight face. It didn't last long and the two of us broke out into a string of laughter. "I told you, bro. She has my head all sorts of messed up."

"Clearly," he agreed as he shook his head at me. His expression was a mixture of confusion and amusement. "I still can't believe you're really taking these lessons right now. Who are you and what have you done with my brother?"

Silence settled around us as I directed my attention out to the beach beneath where we sat. The sound of the ocean slid against my eardrums as the water lapped the shore. Maybe learning ASL was the wrong move. I didn't want to come on too strong. I just wanted to be accommodating to her. I wanted to be able to really talk to her.

Adrian was right. This was completely out of character for me. I never gave much effort before because relationships were always so fleeting. It was hard for me to invest time in people with the way I lived my life. Giana Cirone, though... she was completely different.

"Is it too much?"

Adrian cocked a questioning eyebrow. "Is what too much?"

"Learning ASL. She's not going to be weirded out by it, is she?"

My brother laughed again and I wanted to push him over the railing of the deck. "This is quite amusing. Mr. I'm So Sure of Myself is really questioning everything lately."

"Don't be a dick," I said as I pushed my fingers through my wavy hair. "I just don't want to scare her off."

"If you haven't already, I think you're probably in the clear."

Adrian pushed his chair away from the table and rose to his feet. "I have to head over to Gabriel's practice to talk to him about some of the players." He lifted his mug from the table. "Did you need a ride to your PT appointment? You can come along with me, if you want."

I shook my head, declining his offer. "I appreciate it but I have some errands I need to run while I'm out."

It was bullshit. I didn't have a single errand to run and he knew that, but he didn't call me on it. There was a part of me that just wanted to be by myself. My physical therapy appointment wasn't for another two hours. I could use the time to work on the stuff Mark taught me today. I already went out for a swim this morning and did some of my exercises, so there wasn't much else for me to do.

"I'll catch up with you later then," my brother told me before he disappeared back inside his condo. My eyes found their way back out to the ocean again. I stared out into the distance, watching the way the waves curled and crashed against the sand. There wasn't much force behind them, but they were still mesmerizing.

My mind drifted back to Giana's eyes that matched the color of the ocean. I knew I shouldn't have been trying to start anything with her. Once my shoulder was healed, I would be going back to Malibu. I had a life there and my surfing career was waiting for me. I had no choice but to go back eventually.

As much as I was enjoying my time here, it was just supposed to be a visit. Going back was always what I planned on doing. I didn't come here with the intentions of being swept away by the waves in her ocean-colored eyes. Giana was never part of my plan, but now

I found myself caught in her undertow. I should let her be, let her live her life without me interrupting it all.

I couldn't do that; it was already far too late.

I should walk away now, before either of us ended up developing some type of an attachment to each other. But that was all complete bullshit. I was simply feeding myself lies if I thought there wasn't an attachment formed already. I couldn't walk away from this now. When it came time for me to return to the West Coast, I would worry about that then.

For now, I had two things on my mind.

Giana and getting back on my surfboard so I could ride the waves.

Although, as much as I loved surfing, it felt like it was losing some of its luster. The ocean still called to me and surfing was my entire life. There was a weird shift. It didn't shine as brightly as it once did. In a way, it felt like surfing was beginning to slide into the back seat of my mind.

And Giana was beginning to occupy more space inside my head than anything else.

CHAPTER TEN
GIANA

Moving through the facility, I did my rounds through each building. I was given a list of small tasks in the morning that needed to be completed. Most of them involved feeding and just a brief assessment. Grabbing the clipboard by every tank, I jotted down their overall appearances. Nothing looked out of the ordinary, so I had no abnormal findings to report.

Pop-Tart was the one I had saved for last. Even if I could speak, she couldn't understand a word I would say. It was almost as if we had a weird connection. A nonverbal one. I did my best to not disturb her, but I enjoyed the silence with her. She typically floated around her pool, simply watching me as I stood with my own thoughts swirling around my brain.

She was healing well. Her progress had been great so far and Crew was expecting her to make a full recovery. She still had a ways to go before we would be able to release her, but it was looking extremely promising. The thought alone brought me joy.

I would have never wanted us to release an animal that wouldn't survive back into the wild, but moments like these were the best. The ocean was where she belonged. Where she could be in her natural habitat and be free. Knowing that was in her future brought me a sense of hope that wove itself through my veins.

There was work waiting for me in the lab, but I found myself lingering by Pop-Tart's tank. She was a gentle creature and peace radiated from her. I was forever grateful Declan found her that morning. Her injuries were relatively severe. Had he not found her, chances were she wouldn't have made it. Or she would have lost a flipper, which would have condemned her to living the rest of her days in a tank.

Crew and his team were able to completely remove the fishing line and do a full repair that saved her flipper. She would have residual scarring, but it wouldn't affect her ability to swim. It wouldn't affect her in the least bit, except for cosmetically.

She had a battle scar of her own; she was a goddamn survivor.

As I continued to watch her, my phone vibrated in my back pocket and I pulled it out to see who it was. I smiled to myself when I saw it was Declan.

DECLAN

Hey you. How late do you work today?

The butterflies in my stomach came to life. It had been two days since we last spoke. I was beginning to think maybe he wasn't serious about wanting to see me again because he never showed up after that.

GIANA

I'm here until five or six.

DECLAN

Perfect. I was going to come by and see you and Pop-Tart.

I smiled at the sentiment in his message.

GIANA

We'll be here.

DECLAN

I'll see you later then.

———

The day felt like it was dragging. It was almost as if time had slowed down and the clock was ticking slower than it ever had before. But then it did that weird thing where all of a sudden it caught up. The next thing I knew, it was close to four o'clock and Anna was popping her head through the doorway of the lab.

I looked up from my work in front of me. She

stepped inside, but hovered close by the door. "Someone is here to see you. Do you want me to tell him you'll be out or what?"

I shook my head, grabbed my notepad, and jotted down my response. Anna only knew small pieces of ASL, so it was easier to just write it to her.

You can bring him back here.

She raised a suspicious eyebrow at me. It wasn't a typical thing we did here, but if Declan wanted to help out around here, he was going to have access to everything in the back anyway. I nodded at her.

"I'll send him back."

I watched after her for a moment as she disappeared from the room. My heart was already skipping a beat at the mere thought of him being in the same space as me. My hair was pulled back in a low bun. I was wearing a pair of jeans, a t-shirt, and a lab coat. I didn't really dress to impress today, and it's not like the animals here really cared about my appearance.

Suddenly, I had wished I dressed a little differently today. Or at least put on some makeup or something.

I closed my notebook where I was recording my findings and organized the different tools at my work station. It was a bit of a cluttered mess. I was just looking through some of the samples I took from one of the dolphins we had, searching for evidence of potential pollution effecting its protective layer of skin.

Rising to my feet, I began to clean things up and I was carrying a tray over to the refrigerator just as the door to the lab opened once again. Declan was by himself, looking just as good as he always did. The oxygen from the room instantly vanished and my lungs constricted. He was dressed differently than the last few times I had seen him.

He wore a long-sleeve white SPF shirt that said Riviera Maya across the front in bold navy letters. His wasn't wearing the typical board shorts I usually saw him in. Instead, he was wearing a simple pair of cognac-colored cargo shorts. The door shut behind him and I offered him a smile as he stepped into my space.

I set the tray inside the fridge and turned back around to face him. He lifted his hand to wave at me and I watched his lips move as he said hi. I shifted my weight nervously on my feet and gave him the most awkward wave ever.

And then something completely unexpected happened.

He placed both fists together with his thumbs up and rolled his hands forward so his palms were facing upward with his fingers slightly curled in. He then finished by pointing at me.

"How are you?"

The air left my lungs and my throat constricted. The simple movements of his hands shook me to my core.

He had just signed to me.

My heart literally stopped in my chest. My breath hitched. I stared back at him as a wave of emotion washed over me. Words would never come close to touching the way he had made me feel with one simple sentence.

I swallowed roughly over the emotion that was thick in my throat. Lifting the tips of my fingers on my right hand to my lips, I pulled them away, the back of my hand touching my left palm. *"Good,"* I signed back to him.

His face cracked into a smile, revealing the dimples in his cheeks. "I can't promise I can have a full conversation in ASL, but I know a thing or two."

I was momentarily speechless. My eyes refused to leave his. *"Since when?"* I signed to him.

"After we went to breakfast that one morning." He paused for a moment and ran his fingers through his tousled waves. "I know we have other ways we can communicate, but I want to learn the way you speak. I don't want you to have to write or type everything out all the time. I just want things to be easy for you."

Words failed me. My lips parted and hung open as my gaze was cemented to his golden brown eyes. I couldn't look away. I couldn't blink. Couldn't breathe. He was learning it for *me*. It was the greatest gesture I had ever received from someone. I couldn't accept it, though.

I shook my head at him. *"You don't have to do that."*

"I know I don't," he said matter-of-factly. I was more amazed at the fact that he could understand what I was signing. Or else he was piecing it together based on certain words he could pick out. "I want to, Giana. For once, please just let someone else do something for you."

His words were like a bolt of electricity to my spinal cord. They fissured, the shock dispersing itself throughout my body. He may not have known me long enough to know, but he had been able to make his own conclusions since meeting me. And damn him for being right.

I didn't like help from others. I didn't like people trying to accommodate my needs. I appreciated anyone who took the time to learn ASL so it was easier to communicate, but I also didn't mind handwriting and typing things. It was something I had grown accustomed to. I preferred my independence. The sense that I didn't need anyone for anything and I sure as hell didn't need them treating me any differently or like they needed to shape themselves for me.

Declan extended his left hand with his palm facing the ceiling. His movements were sharp as he opened his right hand and brought it down to his left palm at a ninety-degree angle. *"Stop."*

My eyebrows pulled together and I raised both hands with my palms facing upward as I shook them. *"What?"*

"Get out of your head, princess," he said with simplicity as he closed the distance between us. He stopped as his toes reached mine. I tilted my head back to look up at him. "Stop overthinking everything. If I didn't want to learn, I wouldn't."

Pulling my lips between my teeth, I nodded as I released it. Specks of green and gold swirled in Declan's light eyes. I was close enough that I could count them. He was just within my reach and I balled my hands into fists in an effort to resist reaching out for him. There was something about him that was drawing me in. I was slowly being sucked into his vortex.

He pointed both of his pointer fingers forward. He formed a *D* on both hands with his fingers and tapped them together. They were tilted forward slightly, almost at an angle. My gaze collided with his as he lifted his eyebrows and pointed at himself.

"Go on dessert with me."

My eyebrows pulled together. I pointed at him, turned my hands so they were palm-up, and curled my fingers toward me. I made the sign for dessert, tapping the two *D*'s together twice at an angle. Forming a *Y* on each hand, I bent my elbows with my hands by my face and lowered them toward the ground with my palms facing the ceiling. *"You want dessert now?"*

Confusion laced itself through Declan's expression. "Fuck," he mouthed in frustration. "I'm confused."

I quickly grabbed a piece of paper from my desk and the pen moved fluidly across the surface. *You said to go on dessert with you.*

Declan closed his eyes momentarily before he set the paper down and looked back at me. "I was trying to say go on a *date* with me."

My heart was racing in its cage. My breathing had

picked up and I could feel the butterflies in my stomach as a pit of warmth was building.

I lifted my hands, making two *D*'s. I held them upright with my pointer fingers pointing directly at the ceiling. I tapped my other fingers together twice. "Date," I mouthed simultaneously.

Keeping my fingers in the same shape, I tilted my hands to face him, more at an angle. I tapped them together twice. "Dessert," I moved my lips with the sign.

Declan slid his tongue along the inside of his cheek. "Well, shit," he said as his shoulders deflated. "I really butchered that, huh?"

A smile pulled on my lips. *"Ask me again."*

His throat bobbed as he swallowed, biting back a smile even though those damn dimples refused to be concealed. His eyes glimmered and he signed the words to me again, this time using the correct sign.

"Go on a date with me."

I pulled my bottom lip between my teeth and nodded. *"Okay."*

His grin was earth-shattering as it spread across his face. *"Okay."*

CHAPTER ELEVEN
DECLAN

As I pulled up in front of Giana's building, she was standing there waiting for me. Her long midnight-colored hair hung down her back in cascading waves. She had it pulled away from her face, with a few pieces framing it. The soft breeze blew the wisps of hair across her face as I stepped out of my car and walked over to her.

She was wearing a yellow dress that stopped mid-thigh, looking fucking delectable. It was her color, the perfect contrast against her features. Her bright blue eyes shined back at me as I walked up to her. She walked down the steps and we met at the bottom.

"You steal the air straight from my lungs," I said softly as I closed the small amount of space between us. My fingers slid against her silky skin as I pushed the stray tendrils of hair away from her face. "You look beautiful."

A pink tint crept across her cheeks and a smile broke out across her lips. She lifted her hand, touching her chin with her fingertips before pulling her hand away, her palm facing upward. *"Thank you."*

"Shall we?" I asked as I motioned toward the Jeep. I made sure to put the top back on before picking her up, just in case she didn't want it to mess up her hair.

Giana nodded and she stepped around me before stepping closer to the vehicle. My strides were longer than hers and I reached the door before her. She waited, a shy smile still on her lips as I pulled it open for her and helped her inside.

Her apartment was right along the beach, so we took the main road that led into a busier part of town. It was technically off-season in Orchid City, since most tourists flocked here when it was colder in other parts of the country. This past week, however, had left streets relatively crowded and most of the locals were dining at the restaurants.

Regardless of whether there were tourists or not, the weekends were always busy around here. I wasn't sure what type of food Giana liked, so I picked Huxley's Grill. They were known for their fresh fish and according to Google, they also had a wide range of food that catered to people who didn't enjoy seafood. I wasn't sure if Giana liked seafood or not, especially with her views on the ocean and what humans were doing to it.

It was hard to find a restaurant along the coast that didn't serve seafood.

Their parking lot was full and I circled around before pulling back out onto the street. There was an open spot about a block away. After putting the car in park and killing the engine, I quickly hopped out. Giana was just about to open her door when I reached it. She shook her head with a playful look in her eye. I held my hand out to her to help her out, and there was no hesitation as she slid her warm palm against mine.

I helped her onto the ground, but after she was steady on her feet, I made no move to release her hand. My fingers slid between hers and she curled her fingers around my hand. My heart pounded against my rib cage and a ball of fire built in the pit of my stomach. I wasn't sure if she would pull away, but instead she settled into the comfort between us.

Hand in hand, we fell in step beside one another as we walked down the busy street to Huxley's. I called earlier to make a reservation as soon as Giana agreed to go on a date with me. We were lucky to be able to get in tonight as I managed to grab the last reservation they had available. Giana stayed beside me with her hand in mine as I led her through the restaurant to our table.

It was tucked away on their back deck, in the corner that provided a little bit of privacy and a more intimate feel. The sun was beginning to set to the west and they had strings of lights hanging from above. A small candle was burning on our table and I pulled out Giana's seat for her before she sat down.

The host left menus on the table with promises that our server would be by soon. I thanked him, pushed Giana's seat in, and then took the one directly across from her. Her bright blue eyes were on mine and she adjusted herself in her seat momentarily as she lifted up the menu. I studied her for a moment, my breath caught in my throat as I watched the way her eyes scanned the page in front of her.

It almost felt surreal, sitting here across from her in this moment. She was slowly working her way under my skin. She was already cemented inside my mind, and being around her was the only way to satisfy the craving my soul had for her. It was a strange phenomenon. I had never felt so connected to someone on a spiritual level. I wasn't quite sure how to explain it, but I could feel it deep within the fibers of my soul, and that was the only thing that mattered.

When our server arrived, I was about to order for Giana, but she shook her head at me. Her jaw was set and a storm was brewing in her eyes. She lifted her chin, her eyes meeting the girl standing by our table. She pointed to a cocktail she wanted on the menu along with the food she had chosen. I ordered mine after Giana and our server disappeared from the table.

Giana's stormy eyes were instantly on mine. She pulled out her phone and began to type away on it. I was momentarily thankful because even though I had learned some sign language, there was still a lot I didn't know. And judging by the look of irritation on Giana's face, she was going to have a lot to say.

GIANA

> I appreciate you trying to be helpful, but I don't need you to speak for me. I have my own ways of communicating with people who don't know ASL. And I was honestly doing quite fine with it before you arrived.

Damn. She stared at me with such intensity that her words hit my chest with force. Instantly, there was regret on my part. I wasn't trying to overstep in any way, but it seemed like it made things easier for her the last time we went out.

"I'm sorry," I told her, my voice quiet as I ignored the noise of the restaurant around us. "I just assumed it would be easier if I told her what you wanted. That way you didn't have to deal with it yourself."

She lifted the phone, her fingers moving with lightning speed across the screen before she showed it to me again. There was a flash of anger, hurt and sadness, all mixing together within her irises.

GIANA

> You assumed. You didn't even bother to ask me. You just decided to take it upon yourself to speak for me.

I swallowed roughly over the lump that lodged

itself within my throat. I had clearly offended her, which was not my intention at all. I wasn't quite sure how to proceed. I tilted my head to the side as I watched her expression settle and soften. She pulled the phone back to herself.

"You're right," I admitted as a breath of defeat escaped me. "I shouldn't have assumed and I didn't mean to offend you. It was insensitive of me, and the last thing I want to do is make you feel uncomfortable. From here on out, I will follow your lead, Giana."

She shook her head. Her shoulders hung low in something that resembled guilt.

GIANA

I don't need you to follow my lead. I just need you to ask next time. I spent many years having other people speak for me and if I can help it, I don't let it happen anymore. I prefer my independence and my own voice, even if it is a little different than how others communicate.

I reread her words three times for good measure, letting them seep in as I stared at the screen. I can't imagine what life must have been like for her. To live in her shoes, to experience the tragedy of losing your sense of hearing. To then learn a different way of communicating that most people don't understand, only to have others try to speak for you like you lost your own voice.

"I promise I will never take your voice from you,

princess," I told her as the honesty tangled itself within my words. She couldn't hear my words, but I hoped she could still feel the intensity and the way I fucking meant them. My expression was soft, my eyes desperately searching hers. "Your voice will always be yours and if you ever need me to help you with something, I will let you tell me."

A ragged breath escaped her and the smallest smile danced across her lips. She nodded, lifting her fingertips to her chin before pulling them away. *"Thank you."*

I smiled back at her, just as our drinks were brought over to the table. There wasn't a part of me that was offended or bothered by her speaking her mind. It was exactly what I wanted from her. I wanted her to call me out on my shit, to put me in my place if she felt like I needed it. I wanted the soft and gentle side of Giana Cirone, along with the treacherous storms inside her that sent the waves crashing violently against the shore.

There was a side to her that stood tall and refused to let anyone knock her down.

I wanted every side of her.

The tension in the air between us began to dissipate and Giana changed the subject as she began to ask about my shoulder and surfing. I told her I wanted her to sign everything to me. I wanted to learn every fucking thing I could. A playfulness danced in her eyes and she agreed happily. Her shoulders shook with silent laughter as I struggled along with the conversation and she tried explaining different signs to me.

It was one thing learning from Mark, but learning from Giana was an experience of its own. Our food arrived at the table and we broke the conversation to dive in. I had learned to grow comfortable in the silence that settled between us. I couldn't help myself as my eyes kept colliding with Giana's. A ghost of a smile played on her lips as she caught me watching her every damn time.

As the night was drawing to an end, we were back in my Jeep, heading back to her apartment. I wasn't ready for the night to be over, but all things eventually came to an end. The night with her was simply divine. It was heavenly—more than I could have ever imagined. I knew this wasn't the end of anything between us. It was the beginning.

I wanted to see more of her. And more often.

It wouldn't be long before I would have to head west again... but I couldn't occupy those thoughts. Not now. Not when I was driving through the summer night with Giana's hand in mine.

As I pulled up in front of her building, she slowly released my hand and undid her seat belt before turning to face me.

"Thank you for tonight," she signed and mouthed the words as I was trying to learn them. *"I really did have a good time with you."*

The corners of my lips twitched. "Can I walk you to the door?"

Her gaze lifted from my mouth back to my eyes as

she nodded her head. I left the Jeep running because I didn't want her to think I had any bad intentions. If the engine was still running then I wasn't anticipating her inviting me inside. As much as I wanted her to, I needed her to do that on her terms. I never was one to push others, and I certainly wasn't about to become that person tonight.

Giana waited patiently in the passenger seat as I walked around to open her door for her. I held my hand out to her, almost out of habit, and there was no hesitation as she placed hers in mine. I helped her out of the Jeep, but as her feet touched the ground, she didn't let go of me. I walked her up to the front door and she turned to face me.

"Do you want to come in?" she asked me.

I smiled and shook my head. "Not tonight, princess."

Rejection washed over her expression and I watched a wave of hurt flash through her eyes. She took a step back, releasing my hand and lacing her fingers together in front of her body. It was a defense mechanism. She chewed on the inside of her cheek once and her throat bobbed as she swallowed. *"Okay,"* she mouthed the word. Her chest expanded as she inhaled deeply and met my eyes once more. *"Good night."*

She began to turn her body away from me but I quickly closed the distance between us. It took me two and a half strides to reach her. My hand reached out to grab her shoulders just as she was facing the other direction. I spun her around to face me, her breath hitching as she tilted her head to look up at me. We were standing so close, I could feel the heat radiating from her body.

"I'm trying to be a gentleman here, Giana," I said softly as I lifted my hand from her shoulder and slid it around the back of her neck. Her hair was soft, like silk, and I plunged my fingers through her thick locks as I clutched the back of her head. "Don't test my resolve. It won't take much to break it."

A fire burned deep within the depths of her blue eyes. *"What if I don't want you to be a gentleman?"*

A chuckle vibrated in my chest. "Let me make this clear to you, princess. You're already under my skin, running rampant through my veins. Once I have my way with you, you're mine. I promise you that I will fuck up your life."

She wrapped her arms around my back and pulled me flush against her body. My face was just hovering above hers. *"I hope you follow through on that promise because I look forward to your destruction,"* she mouthed the words slow enough for me to read her lips. *"I want you to ruin me for anyone else."*

"That would be my pleasure, princess," I murmured as I dropped my mouth a fraction closer to hers. "I always make good on my promises, but it won't be happening tonight."

Her lips parted to argue, but I silenced her as I captured her mouth with my own. Her hands fisted my shirt as she clung to me. Her warm body was pressed against mine and I inhaled the scent of honey and lavender as my tongue slid across the seam of her lips. My fingers were tangled in her silky hair as I held her against me. I was the one who initiated the kiss, but it felt as if I was being dragged into the depths of her ocean.

I wasn't sure I would ever resurface. She parted her lips and my tongue slid against hers. I wasn't sure I ever did want to resurface. Her hands gripped my shirt tighter. My cock throbbed against her body that was flush with mine, slowly melting into me. I wanted to fucking drown in her.

Giana's mouth moved with mine. Our lips were fused together, our surroundings had vanished. Her body was fusing with mine and I clung to her with the same ferocity she had. She was like sand on the beach and I was afraid if I loosened my grip, she would slip through my fingers. I wouldn't let that happen, not if I could help it.

Our tongues were tangled in one another. Her throat was exposed, her head tilted back as she let me in. I swallowed her murmurs and breathed her in. My lungs were filled to the brim with her. She was everywhere. Giana Cirone wasn't just under my skin.

She was embedded in my fucking soul.

And I was already drowning in her.

CHAPTER TWELVE

GIANA

The water lapped at my waist and my body swayed with the waves as I dug my toes into the wet ocean floor. Granules of sand were pinched between my toes, scratching at my skin. The ocean was warm and the sun was shining brightly in the sky above. I looked out across the surface, watching the way it glimmered beneath the light.

Declan was to the side of me, trying to position his surfboard for me to get on. He wasn't cleared by his doctor to be able to physically surf yet, but that didn't keep him from the water. He was either out here swimming or absentmindedly floating around on his board. Declan didn't strike me as one to do anything to jeopardize the healing process of his injury, but then again, it seemed a little suspicious that he would even bother bringing his surfboard out here.

After our date last week, he made it clear he wasn't

going anywhere. He wanted more time with me and I agreed because it was mutual. There was something about him that was constantly pulling me in. He had his grip on me and I didn't want him to let go anytime soon. Work was busy this past week and he had a bunch of appointments, so it was hard to coordinate our schedules, but today was a new day. I requested the day off and Declan insisted on trying to teach me how to surf.

It was as hard as it looked.

"Hold on to the board," Declan instructed me as he moved to the other side of it and pushed it in front of me. "Lean across it and use your weight to propel yourself onto it."

I stared at him for a moment. Any attempts I had made in the past were futile and it was in much shallower water, where I could easily straddle the board. Now he wanted me to lift myself up onto it in the water that was constantly shifting us around.

This was going to be a disaster.

How was he even going to show me how to surf when he couldn't do it himself?

I followed his instructions while he held the board for me to keep it from floating away. My body didn't really weigh that much but it felt like it when I threw my body across the board. My stomach was pressed against the cool surface and I slid the length of my body along the length of the board.

"Straddle it, princess." The flames in his eyes

burned brighter and I wondered how he sounded when he spoke those words out loud. I imagined them sounding husky and full of lust. "Sit on the board."

"Okay," I mouthed back to him as I nodded. I could do this. I planted my palms on the board and slid my legs down into the water on either side. I slowly pushed myself up until I was sitting upright. I looked down at Declan and he smiled brighter than the damn sun as he looked up at me through his sunglasses.

His hair was wet from the salt water. The tips glistened and droplets fell onto his perfectly tanned, perfectly sculpted shoulders. Declan Parks was a literal work of art. There wasn't a single piece of him that wasn't carved to perfection. My eyes traced the shape of his lips and the Cupid's bow in his top lip just as a wave pushed the board with an extra ounce of force. My gaze flashed to his, my eyes widening as my breath escaped me in a rush.

Declan's one hand was still clutching the surfboard and the other went directly to my thigh. His touch burned my skin. His hands were conflicting and contradictory. Soft and gentle, yet rough and hard. He held on to me, his fingers digging into my flesh as he steadied me and the board.

"It's okay, princess," his lips formed the words, "I got you."

My heart was pounding erratically in my chest, thumping harder and harder against my rib cage. There was a rush of adrenaline from the ocean giving me a momentary scare, but the reaction was really from him. From the way his hand was molded to my own flesh. And the way I didn't want him to move it away from me.

His eyes were still trained on mine.

"Don't let go," I mouthed the words to him as I signed them. I had since let go of the surfboard and the worst that would happen was I would fall into the water. *"I don't know what I'm supposed to do."*

Declan huffed and his brow furrowed in frustration. "This would be a lot easier if I could physically show you." He slowly turned the board around so I was facing the shore. "We're going to start out slow. I'll show you what I can and as soon as my doctor gives me the okay, I'll show you everything I can."

I nodded my head, my heart still pounding to its own beat inside my chest. *"What now?"*

"Look behind you," he said, pointing out to the ocean with the hand that wasn't on my thigh. He was still holding on to me. "You see the way the water curls as it crawls closer to the shoreline? It turns white as it breaks and rolls toward the beach. The next one that has a little more definition to it, I want you to ride it."

My eyes widened and I shook my head at him. *"I don't know how."*

He smiled at me. "Don't worry, princess. You're not ready to stand up and ride it. I'm not going to send you on a suicide mission, although the waves here are laughable in comparison to the ones in other places."

I narrowed my eyes at him, my lips parting as I was about to mouth something back to him. Something most definitely snarky, but he cut me off as his hands slid up to my waist.

"Lay on your stomach, princess," he told me as he gently urged me forward. I lifted my legs from the water, stretching my body out along the length of the board as I clutched the sides of it. "Start paddling to shore and when the wave reaches you, just hold on to the board and ride it in."

I stared at him with a wild look in my eyes as I shook my head again. Declan was already removing his hands from my waist and taking a step backward. *What are you doing? Why did you let me go?"*

He flashed his perfect white teeth at me. "You can do this, I know you can. Here comes the wave." He winked at me and gave me a thumbs-up.

I cut my eyes at him once more before directing my gaze ahead of me. The anxiety had begun to creep in and my breathing had picked up. I followed his instructions and began to paddle toward the shore, even though I wanted to hop off. The wave reached the back of the board and I felt it lift slightly. Pulling my arms back out of the water, I clutched the sides of the surfboard just as the wave was pushing me toward the beach.

Adrenaline spiked in my system, running fluidly through my body as I let the ocean take charge. It wasn't violent or scary like I had imagined. The ocean air was sticking to my face, simultaneously pushing my hair back as I rode the wave in. It lost its momentum, slowing as I coasted farther into the shallow waters. It pushed me up onto the beach, the sand scraping my hands as I moved up and out of the water.

I was still on my stomach, but the surfboard was stuck, like a beached sea animal. I released the sides of it and pushed myself up to a sitting position just as I caught movement from the corner of my eye. Slowly turning around, still seated upon the board, my eyes were stuck on Declan. He was walking out of the water, his body dripping wet and the dimples prominent in his cheeks. My eyes traveled across the perfectly chiseled planes of his abdomen. Over every dip and curve of the muscles of his athletic body.

My mouth instantly felt dry as a ball of heat was building in my stomach. The effect he had on me, I wasn't sure if I should welcome it with my arms wide open or run in the opposite direction. He scared me and sent a thrill through me in the same breath.

"You did so good." He smiled down at me as he paused by the side of the board. The sun was behind him, creating an outline of luminosity around his body. He was ethereal. Undeniably beautiful. "I told you, you could do it."

I scooted backward a bit, making room for him on the board as he lifted one leg over it. He sat down, straddling the surfboard with his legs stretched out. He lifted his sunglasses from his face, not caring as he tossed them onto the sand beside us. Leaning forward, his hands found my hips and he pulled me toward him. He didn't stop until my body was flush against his, my legs bent over his thighs.

His fingertips were damp and cold from the ocean as he ran them across the side of my face. He pulled a strand of hair between his fingers before tucking it behind my ear. Declan trailed his fingers along the side of my jaw before flattening his palm against my neck. His thumb pressed under my chin to tilt my head back.

"What are you doing, Declan?" I mouthed the words to him as my hands ran over his bare skin, wrapping around his back.

His eyes danced under the light of the sun. "I want to taste the ocean on your lips, princess."

My eyelids fluttered shut as his breath skated across my face. I inhaled deeply, breathing in the scent of him. He smelled like the sea and the sun and I was entirely lost in him. His lips moved across mine with a tenderness as his fingers curled around the back of my neck. There was nothing rushed or urgent with how he kissed me. He kissed me like time ceased to exist. Like it was an illusion. Like it was ours and no one else's. His mouth melted into mine and he tasted like the ocean and mint.

As his tongue slid against mine, the fire ignited between us. His other hand was gripping my waist, pulling me as close as he could get me. His erection pressed against my center, with only the fabric of our bathing suits separating us. Shifting my hips the slightest bit, I rubbed against him, craving the friction. A moan vibrated from Declan's chest, racking my entire body.

The flames were ablaze and there was a shift between us. Dropping his hand away from my face, both of his hands gripped my waist, lifting me onto his lap. A ragged breath escaped me and now I was hovering above him. My hands found his shoulders and I trailed my fingers across them before moving them along the nape of his neck.

His hair was wet, a tousled mess of waves, and I tangled my hands within them as he stared up at me with his golden brown eyes. A soft breath slipped from his perfect lips just before I dropped mine back to his. His fingertips were digging into my skin and I gripped his hair tighter as his tongue slid into my mouth.

We were caught up in one another, completely consumed. It didn't matter that there were other people on the beach. In that moment, the only thing that mattered was the two of us.

Declan stole the air from my lungs and left me breathless before he abruptly pulled away. "I'm done being a gentleman, Giana."

My tongue slid against my own lips, tasting him and the sea on them. They were swollen from how he kissed me. *What changed?*

"You," he said as he lifted his hands to cup the sides of my face. "You changed everything."

"I need you, Declan."

His throat bobbed, his eyes burned deeply. "I told you what happens if we enter this territory."

"Take me back to your place," I moved my lips to form the words slow enough for him to read them. I lifted myself from his lap and grabbed his hand to pull him with me. Declan rose to his feet, his eyes searching mine as he stared down at me, looking for assurance. I lifted up onto my toes, my lips moving against his. *"Now."*

I dropped back down to find that his eyes were a mixture of emotions I couldn't quite dissect. His hand found mine, and he bent down to pick up his board with his other hand before tucking it under his arm.

"Come with me, princess."

CHAPTER THIRTEEN
DECLAN

The walk to my brother's house felt like it was the longest walk of my life, even though it was only a little under two minutes. Giana's hand was in mine and I was holding my surfboard with my good arm. I wanted to feel her flesh beneath my hands, her skin beneath my mouth. I wanted to touch her, to taste her, to please her the way she deserved to be pleased. The fire between us was burning brighter than the sun and it was taking everything in me to restrain myself from pushing her up against the garage door.

Instead, I set my surfboard down and punched in the code to open the door. Giana and I waited for it to open completely. I left my board inside the garage before pulling Giana into the house with me.

Thankfully my brother was at work for the day, doing God knows what. Even though he was the

Orchid City Vipers' team doctor, he worked with the team when they weren't playing. In the summer, he was still busy working with the different hockey players. I wasn't sure of the specifics of his job, but I just knew he was gone most of the day—and that was perfectly fine with me.

Giana's eyes traveled around the open floor plan. All the walls were painted white and there were a few pieces of art my brother bought from different charity events at the local country club. I spun her toward me, pulling her until her body was flush against mine. She tilted her head back to look at me.

"Your brother?"

I shook my head at her, bending my knees slightly as I dropped her hand and slid mine down to grab her thighs just beneath her ass. "He won't be home until this evening."

She inhaled sharply as I lifted her into the air. Instinctively, her legs wrapped around my waist. She linked her hands behind the back of my neck as a smile pulled on her lips. *"Perfect."*

God, she was perfect.

My bedroom was on the first floor and I carried her straight into my room. Holding her in my arms, I kicked the door shut behind me. Giana slid her fingers through my hair and I paused to look at her. Lust and need washed over her ocean blue irises. Her mouth inched closer to mine. My grip tightened on her thighs, just as her lips grazed mine.

It was game fucking over.

She kissed me slowly with such an unyielding tenderness. It was torturous and tantalizing and I wanted more of her. I wanted *all* of her. My eyelids fell shut as she breathed me in. She took control, her soft lips moving gently against mine. There wasn't any hesitation, but she also wasn't in a hurry. Giana Cirone was taking her sweet time torturing me.

My feet didn't stop blindly moving until my knees were hitting the side of the mattress. I lowered her down onto the bed without breaking away from her. Her legs fell away from my body and we moved together as I crawled onto the mattress with her, the two of us moving toward the center of the bed. Lifting my face from hers, I stared down at her. Her midnight-colored hair was splayed out across the white comforter, still damp from the ocean water.

My breath caught in my throat as she stared up at me with her soft eyes.

Goddamn, she was absolutely fucking beautiful.

My eyes trailed across her naked torso. She was wearing nothing but the light blue bikini she had on at the beach. Just scraps of fabric were separating us. Giana watched me as I unapologetically drank in the sight of her. She sat up, reaching behind her back. My eyes met hers as she undid the straps to her bikini and pulled it away from her body. It fell onto the bed beside her.

A ragged breath escaped me. "You're a piece of art,"

I whispered hoarsely as she laid back on the bed. I leaned toward her, running my fingertips along her collarbone. She shivered as I slid them to the center of her chest and dragged them through the valley between her perfect breasts. "The most beautiful piece I've ever laid eyes on."

Her slender throat bobbed as she swallowed. Her gaze was trained on mine. My mouth went dry as she slid her hands beneath the strings of her bikini bottoms. Wetting my lips with my tongue, I watched her as she pushed them down her thighs and past her feet before tossing them onto the floor. She was completely naked, lying on my bed waiting for me.

Jesus Christ.

Her hands reached for the waistband of my board shorts. My cock was already harder than fucking stone and it was throbbing against my shorts. She pulled her hands away, pointing at herself as she began to sign to me. *"I want to see you,"* she signed while mouthing the words. *"Take them off."*

Moving off the bed, I did as she asked. I stripped my shorts away, leaving them on the floor as I stepped out of them. Giana scooted more toward the head of the bed. She lifted a finger, a ghost of a smile playing on her lips as she curled it toward herself, motioning for me to come to her.

In that moment, I realized just how far gone I was for this girl. She could have said less than that and I still would have been crawling on my hands and knees across the bed to her. Hell, I'd crawl across hot sand for her if she asked me to.

As I inched closer, lust was dancing in her eyes. I caged her in with my arms on either side of her head and pinned her body to the mattress with the weight of my own. I slid one hand along her neck, slowly curling my fingers around the column of her throat as my mouth collided with hers. She still tasted like the sea. My tongue slid along the seam of her lips and she parted them, letting me in.

Our lips were melting together. Tongues tangling, teeth clashing. It wasn't gentle like it was before. There was nothing but urgency, need. Lust and desire. She wanted every piece of me just as badly as I wanted the same from her.

I kissed her until there was no air left in either of our lungs. Until we were both forced to break apart from one another. To come up for air. She was completely breathless, her chest rising and falling in rapid succession with every ragged breath.

I buried my face in her neck, tasting and nipping at her skin. My body began to move down the length of hers, trailing my lips and tongue across every inch of her skin. Her body quivered under my touch. As I made my way down to the bottom of her stomach, I settled between her legs, gently pushing her thighs apart. I lifted my head, looking up at her to make sure what I was doing was okay.

Her blue eyes were hazy with lust. She raked her

teeth across her bottom lip while slowly running her fingers through the tangled waves on my head. I watched her carefully, counting three erratic heartbeats in my chest before she released her bottom lip and nodded. Her head fell back against the mattress, just as she began to guide my own down between her parted thighs until my breath was grazing across her pussy.

Giana's hands were still in my hair as I buried my face in between her legs. My tongue slipped out of my mouth and I licked her, flattening my tongue against her as I reached her clit. Her entire body lifted from the bed and I couldn't help but smile knowing I did that to her. Her grip tightened on my hair as I pulled her clit between my lips and sucked on it.

The softest whimper escaped her. My heart stopped beating for a moment as I let the sound she made seep into the fibers of my soul. Giana never made a fucking sound, except for now. I wanted it ingrained in my memory for the rest of my goddamn life.

I held her in place as I circled my tongue around her clit before releasing it from my lips. I continued to fuck her with my mouth, licking her pussy before teasing her clit again. I wanted to torture her as badly as she torture me with that kiss she initiated between us. She was officially the prey and I planned on devouring her.

Moving my arms from her thighs, I slid my hands underneath her ass and gripped her cheeks within my fingertips. They dug into her flesh as I held her in place and feasted upon her. Her breath was ragged, the sounds filling the air around us. Jesus, all the little sounds she was making that she didn't even realize. They were for me and me only.

Her body was growing tense beneath my touch, but I wasn't going to stop. I wasn't stopping until she was free falling into the abyss of ecstasy. I wanted nothing more than to drive her as wild as she drove me. She didn't know it, and I had only recently come to the realization of what she was doing to me. This was a game the two of us were now playing.

Her fingers were still in my hair, and my face was still buried between her legs. My tongue moved with precision and swift movements against her, pushing her closer and closer to the edge. I could feel the intensity of her orgasm building without her telling me. My balls were constricting, drawing closer to my own body. I felt like I was going to explode from the pressure that was building within me.

Thrusting my tongue inside her, Giana's hips bucked against my face. She gasped loudly, her fingertips digging into my scalp. I smiled against her pussy as I drove my tongue inside her once more before making my way back to her clit. Releasing one of her cheeks with my hand, I slowly trailed my fingers along her body until I was pressing it against her.

Slipping one finger inside her, I lapped at her clit while I began to fuck her with my hand. I added another, pumping my fingers in and out of her while massaging her insides. Her pussy clenched around me and I kept moving, teasing her clit at the same time.

She inhaled sharply, a soft cry escaping her as the orgasm hit her intensely. Her hips bucked against my face, but I held her down against the bed as I continued to move my fingers and tongue against her.

She was coming apart at the seams, losing herself on my tongue and my fingers.

And I wanted every last drop she had to give.

CHAPTER FOURTEEN
GIANA

My head was in the clouds, my entire body levitating through the air. My eyelids were clamped shut as my orgasm was beginning to subside, but the aftershocks still had my body feeling like it was glowing. I felt his absence immediately as he withdrew his fingers from me and pressed his lips in a soft kiss against my clit. The contact sent an electrical shock through my body.

My vision was hazy as I forced my eyes open and lifted my head to look up at Declan. I was still riding a high that I had never felt before. *"I've never experienced anything like that before,"* I admitted, moving my lips slow enough for him to read them.

A smirk played on his lips as he began to crawl up my body, placing kisses all along my flesh until his mouth met mine. His tongue slid against mine and I could taste myself on him.

He pulled away to look at me. "Has no one ever pleasured you like that before, princess?"

I shook my head at him. I'd been with one other guy before and he was never able to bring me to orgasm. He only ever went down on me once before but it was nothing like what I had just experienced with Declan. I never imagined it to be like that—seeing a million stars while a rush of ecstasy flooded my veins.

Declan tilted his head to the side, a look of curiosity passing through his eyes as he stared down at me. "Has anyone ever made you come before?"

I bit down on my bottom lip and he lifted his hand. His thumb brushed against my lip, pulling it free from my teeth. *"No,"* I mouthed the word to him while shaking my head again. *"Only me."*

His eyes glowed, hues of golden brown and green swirling within them. "I'm honored," he told me as he wet his own lips. A mixture of emotions were building within his irises. "Let me show you just how good I can make you feel, princess."

I couldn't hear the words he spoke, but they vibrated from his chest and through my body. I slid my hands around the back of his neck, pulling his face closer to mine. He stopped abruptly.

"I need to see if my brother has any condoms."

His weight shifted as he started to move away from me, but I didn't let go of him. Instead, I pulled on him, turning his head back to face me. *"Don't,"* I said in my head while mouthing the word. *"I'm on the pill."*

His eyes widened slightly while the fire inside of them threatened to consume his irises completely. "Are you sure?"

I nodded. *"I want to feel you... all of you."*

"Fuck," he breathed. He looked conflicted for a moment, as if he wasn't sure whether or not he was doing the right thing. I hooked my legs around his waist to show him I meant what I had said. His throat bobbed as he swallowed roughly. "Fuck it."

His mouth collided with mine once again, distracting me with his tongue as the tip of his cock pressed against my pussy. I was still wet from his tongue, still wet from my own arousal. He slid into me, and pleasure and pain mixed together as he stretched me wide. His movements were slow and calculated, but he filled me to the brim as he dove in as deep as my body would allow.

Feeling his thick length filling me had me seeing stars again. My eyes threatened to roll back in my head, but I fought against it as his tongue tangled with mine. They were caught in their own sensual dance. He began to shift his hips, slowly moving in and out of me with every thrust.

Sliding my hands down to his shoulders, I clung to him as he began to move his hands down my body. My nails dug into his skin, leaving half-moon shapes in his flesh. He planted one hand on the mattress beside my head as he slid the other beneath my ass, lifting it into the air to get a different angle.

My breath escaped me, my heart beating rapidly in my chest as he began to fuck me harder. His lips broke away from mine and he buried his face in the crook of my neck before tasting and teasing the sensitive skin there. His teeth nipped at my flesh and a whimper slipped from my own lips. I was trying to hold back every sound that was building in my throat but some were just too hard for me to fight against.

I was lost in him, completely caught up in the moment. Nothing else mattered except Declan buried deep inside me with my legs wrapped tightly around his waist. He thrust with such force, it felt like he was going to fuck me through the mattress. I was encapsulated by the silence, only this time, it wasn't just silent. It wasn't just me and my own thoughts.

I could feel the moans and groans vibrating in his chest, vibrating through my own body. The way he felt, moving against me and inside me. It was a silent melody that only the two of us could hear. His skin beneath my fingers. His body pressed against mine. I could hear everything while hearing nothing at all.

His hand abandoned my ass, but he never moved it away from me. He slipped it between both of our bodies, his thumb instantly finding my clit. Bending his opposite elbow, he lowered himself closer to me, sliding his hand around the back of my neck. His lips moved against my ear and I wanted to hear the words he whispered to me.

He knew I couldn't hear them, so instead, he showed me with his body and the way he touched me.

His thumb circled my clit as he continued to pound into me. His lips were moving against the side of my neck, trailing kisses along my skin. Declan continued to thrust harder and harder, pushing me closer to the edge with his cock and his hand. It didn't take long before the warmth was building to the point it felt like it was going to spill over.

And one more stroke of his cock inside me, one last swirl of his thumb, was all it took. The warmth spilled over, flooding my veins as my orgasm hit me with such an intensity, my vision began to grow black as it felt like I was going to pass out. He sent me soaring through the sky, riding a high like one I had never experienced before.

I was shattering into a million pieces around him and he was equally as lost as I was. I couldn't stop the sound as I cried out. My orgasm sent an earthquake tearing through my body. My legs tightened around him, my pussy clenching him tighter than a vise grip. My entire body was on fire as I shook around him with such force.

He sank his teeth into the flesh on my shoulder as his own orgasm consumed him. Rocking into me once more, his chest vibrated from a low moan, vibrating through my own body. The warmth of him filled me instantly, but I was too busy watching the stars floating around my vision to care about it. I meant it when I told him I wanted to feel all of him. I wanted this with him. Something I had never experience with anyone else.

Declan collapsed against me with his cock still deep inside me. I was still riding on a high that I wasn't sure I wanted to come down from. My chest rose and fell with every ragged breath that escaped me as my heart hammered away in my chest. Closing my eyes, I inhaled deeply, breathing in the scent of him. He smelled like the sea and the sun.

My most favorite combination.

He slowly rolled off of me and I instantly felt his absence as he pulled out of me. My eyelids fluttered open and I watched him as he climbed off the bed. His soft eyes met mine. "I'll be right back."

I watched him disappear from the room, through a door that wasn't the one we came in through. It was a bathroom that was attached to his room, and he wasn't gone for long. Less than a minute later, he was back in the room, walking toward me with a washcloth in his hand. He didn't speak a word as he lowered himself onto the bed and pressed the warm, damp cloth against me.

I watched him carefully as he cleaned me up. His eyes met mine again and he gave me a lazy grin before tossing the washcloth over into the laundry basket by his closet. He didn't move from where he was sitting on the edge of the bed.

A lump formed in my throat as I watched his expression morph into a mixture of emotions as his eyes raked over my body. His chest fell as he released a deep breath. His gaze traveled along my skin until it collided with my own. Declan's eyes were soft and warm, filled with so much emotion, it was enough to fill the ocean.

I felt entirely exposed. Flesh and bone, all for him to see. He stared directly into my soul, sending a bolt of lightning down my spine. I didn't want to escape his eyes. I reveled in the way he looked at me.

"You're a goddess, Giana," he said to me as he trailed his fingers along the curves of my body as I rolled onto my side. "Absolutely breathtaking." His fingers slid across my rib cage as he began to lower himself onto the bed beside me. We were laying on the bed, facing one another. He lifted his hand to cup the side of my face with a tenderness that shook me to my core. "You steal the air from my lungs, but I don't even want it back. It's yours to have."

I couldn't breathe. I couldn't form words with my hands or mouth. I simply stared back at him, completely lost within the depths of his golden brown eyes.

And in that moment, I knew...

He was either going to be the best thing or the worst thing that had ever happened to me.

CHAPTER FIFTEEN
DECLAN

Lying in bed with Giana felt surreal. We had spent the greater part of the afternoon wrapped up in one another. I slowly got up, my hand finding hers before dragging her to her feet. Giana followed me into the bathroom and hovered behind me as I turned the water on in the shower. It was hot within an instant. Giana's hand was still in mine and I pulled her inside the glass shower with me.

Grabbing her shoulders, I turned her so her back was to the water, and she took a few steps back. I watched as her eyelids fluttered shut. Her head was tilted so her face was pointed toward the ceiling. I was in complete awe of her. Struck by her beauty. Water penetrated her hair, soaking it as it stretched down the length of her spine, resting just above her ass.

I could stare at her for the rest of eternity and never grow tired of looking at her.

There was a bottle of shampoo sitting on the built-in shelves in the stone walls. I picked it up and squirted some into my hand before turning Giana around to face the opposite direction. My fingers plunged through her hair, massaging her scalp with the shampoo. She leaned her head into my touch, a small moan escaping her lips as I worked my fingertips against her.

I worked it until the lather was rolling down my forearms. Spinning her back around, I washed the shampoo from her hair. She pressed her hands against my chest as she moved out of the water and we traded places. Her hands trailed across my skin. My cock was already hard, but I ignored it as she pulled me back from the stream and was mimicking my actions, massaging shampoo against my scalp.

It was intimate and sensual. The water beat down upon the two of us as we took turns scrubbing one another. After cleaning our hair, I ran a fresh washcloth across every inch of her skin, washing away the ocean and our mess. She did the same, washing my body for me before we both rinsed off.

As I stood under the stream of water, feeling it pelt my back, I reached for her, pulling her naked body flush against mine. Her flesh was wet and slick from the shower. Pushing my hand underneath her hair, I gripped the back of her neck while backing her against the stone wall. My lips found hers in an instant. She kissed me back with fervent need. My tongue plunged inside her mouth, sliding against hers as my other hand gripped her hip.

Giana's arms were around my torso, her nails digging into my back as we took turns stealing the air from one another's lungs. It wasn't long before my hands were gripping the backs of her thighs and I was lifting her into the air. Pressing her against the wall, her hands moved to my shoulders and her legs wrapped around my waist.

Ever so gently, I lowered her down onto me as I sank my cock deep inside her. A breathy moan escaped her as she breathed against my mouth. I swallowed her sounds, my tongue tangling with hers as I held her against the wall. Shifting my hips, I began to piston them, sliding myself in and out of her in calculated, fluid movements.

I would never be able to get enough of this woman.

It wasn't long before I was pounding into her with such force, her teeth were clashing against mine. Not once did either of us come up for air. Our lips were fused to one another's, our sounds melting together as I fucked her harder and harder.

The warmth built inside me as her pussy tightened around the length of my cock. I could feel her orgasm building and as it finally erupted, she pulled me into the abyss of ecstasy with her. She started to come first, but that was what pushed me over the edge. That was what had me coming deep inside her pussy, filling her with my cum a second time.

Giana cried out and I swallowed the sound as I pumped into her once more. Her body was shaking from pleasure and I held her tightly as our bodies rode out the euphoric waves. I broke apart from her and her forehead collapsed against my shoulder as I wrapped my arms around her. Her chest rose and fell in rapid succession, her shallow breaths grazing across my skin.

She slowly lifted her head, her eyes dazed and glossy as she stared down at me with a smile pulling on her lips. It was sleepy and filled with nothing but satisfaction.

"That was unexpected." She moved her lips around the words without making a sound.

My eyes never once left hers as I lowered her feet back onto the shower floor. "I couldn't help myself." I winked at her. "I'm not responsible for how I react to you being in such close proximity."

She blinked, rolling her eyes, while she bit back a smile. *"You're something else."*

And you're everything.

I responded with another wink before the two of us washed up again and slipped out of the shower to dry off. I handed her two towels and we both stepped out of the bathroom and into my bedroom. She moved over to the bed, a frown finding its way onto her lips as she lifted her bikini up. It was the only thing she had with her.

Turning my back to her, I grabbed one of my t-shirts

and basketball shorts. She gave me a quizzical look as I held them out to her.

"You need something to wear," I told her with a shrug. "Just wear these until I take you home."

She stared at me for a moment, her expression unreadable. I wanted inside her mind. I wanted her thoughts for myself. She took the clothes from me. *"Thank you,"* she signed to me while mouthing the words.

My lips parted as I was about to respond, when I heard sound coming from another room in the house. I glanced over at the alarm clock on my nightstand. The time had gotten away from the two of us. For her own privacy and to avoid any awkwardness, I was going to get her home before my brother was home from work.

Too late.

She quickly dressed and I did the same. Our outfits were almost the same and I couldn't help the laugh that bubbled from my chest. Giana couldn't hear the sound, but she saw it and cut her eyes at me while shaking her head.

I stepped closer to her. "You look beautiful, princess." I wrapped my hand around the back of her head, pulling her close as I pressed my lips to her forehead. I moved away, looking back down at her again. "Stay for dinner?"

Her eyebrows pulled together. *"What about your brother?"*

"He may or may not know about you already," I

told her with a wink. "Plus, the two of you kind of know each other."

She looked even more confused. *"How?"*

"He's the Orchid City Vipers' team doctor."

"Adrian Parks?" She spelled his name out with her fingers. Her eyes widened and her mouth formed an O shape. *"Makes sense now."*

I smiled at her while giving my head a subtle shake. Holding my hand out to her, I waited as I motioned toward the bedroom door. I wasn't sure if this was a good or bad idea, but there was no way around it now. I couldn't sneak her out without my brother seeing her… and I wasn't so sure I wanted her to be a secret.

Giana slid her hand into mine, lacing our fingers together. I gave it a small squeeze in reassurance and led her out of my bedroom door and through the house. The smell of taco seasoning and lime filled the air as we headed toward the kitchen. Adrian loved to cook, so I wasn't surprised to find him making dinner already.

"What's up, Aid?" I said to my brother's back as he hovered over the simmering pots and pans on the stove. Giana held on to my hand tightly.

He glanced over his shoulder to me and his eyes widened slightly as he noticed Giana standing beside me. I was sure it was a sight to be seen. The two of us both wearing my clothes, along with our hair still damp from the shower.

"You remember Giana, right?"

Adrian turned around slowly, wiping his hands on

the apron he was wearing. I stifled a laugh as I read the saying on the front. *I'll feed all you fuckers.* He looked between Giana and I with a smile. "Of course I remember her." He looked to her with a softness in his gaze. "I hope you like tacos."

She nodded, her smile matching his as she released my hand. *"I love them,"* she signed to him.

"Perfect," he responded before turning back to the food he was cooking.

My eyebrows were instantly pulling together. "You know sign language?"

Adrian didn't bother looking at me. "Of course I do. I'm well versed in many languages."

I moved to the fridge to get Giana and I both a bottle of water, but when I turned around, I found her wandering over to my brother. Confusion laced itself within my expression as I watched the two of them.

"Do you need any help?" she asked him.

He nodded. "That would be lovely." He handed her one of the spatulas and showed her what he was making before he glanced over at me again. "Dec, why don't you go ahead and set the table for the three of us?"

I mumbled something unintelligible under my breath, huffing in annoyance as I watched my brother and my girl cooking together. Was she my girl? Fuck, I didn't know if that was even a real thing. But it felt like it. In my mind, in my eyes, she was mine and no one else's.

It didn't take long before the three of us were seated at the table and fell into comfortable conversation as we passed the food around to make our own tacos. Adrian asked Giana about her job, telling her that Nico mentioned some of her work to him. He was genuinely intrigued and there was an ease between them that brought me a sense of peace.

I hadn't made the wrong decision, after all.

After dinner, Adrian bid us both a good night before he disappeared into his study. He claimed he had some work to do before heading to bed for the night, but there was a part of me that knew he'd be sneaking off to Pier Six at some point. He had a habit of doing it after leading me to believe he was in for the rest of the evening.

It wasn't my business. What he did was his choice and it didn't concern me.

Giana and I cleaned up the table from dinner and she helped to load the dishwasher while I put stuff in the fridge. It was bizarre and so extremely domesticated. Yet it just felt... right. As we finished up, she turned toward me and I leaned against the counter, studying the freckles splayed across her cheeks.

"It's late," I murmured, my eyes finding hers. "I suppose I should probably get you home."

She took a step toward me. Then another. And another. She closed the gap between us and was standing directly in front of me. Her hand reached out to cup my cheek before trailing her fingers along the side of my jaw. *"Is that what you want to do?"*

"Fuck no," I admitted as I reveled in her touch. The warmth of her fingers against my skin. "If I had it my way, you'd be staying with me tonight."

"What if I told you I didn't want you to take me home?"

My breath lodged in my throat. "You want to stay with me?"

She pulled her bottom lip between her teeth and nodded. I straightened my body upright, pulling her flush against me. My hand slid beneath her chin, tilting her head back to look at me. My lips gently grazed hers before I pulled back again to look into the stormy depths of her irises.

"Heaven knows I don't deserve you, but I'll never stop trying to prove my worth."

The tides between us ceased to exist.

Our mouths collided and we crashed into one another.

Again and again… like the relentless waves crashing against the coast.

Together, we *were* the tide.

CHAPTER SIXTEEN
GIANA

"Who's ready for a round of shots?" Winter giggled as she walked back over to the high-top table, juggling three small shot glasses. She wasn't a big drinker, but since we were having our first girls' night in a little bit, she felt we needed a shot.

Harper sipped her martini and smiled brightly at her. "Hey, why not? If they're coming to the table anyway, I'm not going to turn them down."

My eyes traveled back and forth between the two of them, rapidly reading their lips. It had become second nature over my years of life and came easily to me. They were both conscious of my hearing loss that they signed while speaking to make it easier for me, but it didn't really make much of a difference. As long as my brain was focused and engaged, I could follow along.

But it was equally exhausting, trying to keep up and

constantly process what everyone was saying, whether it was reading the way their mouths formed around words or their words forming with their fingers.

Add in alcohol and things always tended to get a little more muddled.

Winter sat at the other seat at our high-top table and handed Harper and I each a shot. I looked at the pale green liquid in the glass and raised my eyebrows as I looked back to my best friend. *"Green tea shot?"*

"Remember the summer before college?" she started as she spoke aloud while simultaneously signing to me. "That one bartender from the country club came to Eloise Gervais's graduation party because they were sneaking around together and he made them for everyone?"

I stared at her for a moment, my eyebrows pulling together before I burst out into a silent laugh. My shoulders shook and I almost snorted while shaking my head. *"How the hell would I remember that? That was, like, six years ago, and I'm fairly certain I blacked out that night."*

Winter shrugged. "I don't know. I never really drank much and I always remembered them because I liked how they tasted."

"They are good," Harper added with a wink as she took a sip of hers. It was a mixed shot and it seemed to be one most people preferred to drink slower because of the taste.

We all sipped on our small glasses, ignoring the mixed drinks we already had. Harper had already told us all about her recent endeavors with her photography business. Considering the fact that she was dating my brother, I knew enough about their love life that I kind of tuned her out as she clued Winter in on how great their relationship was.

I truly was happy for my brother. I loved Harper. She was great for him and together, they were an amazing couple.

The same was true for Winter and Malakai. They had just gotten home from another trip. If there was one person who would literally burn the entire world to fucking ash for someone, it was Malakai. Winter was the only person who mattered in his life. He didn't care much for anyone but her. And if anything ever happened to her—I'd hate to see the destruction he would cause.

"So, Giana," Harper started to speak and sign with her eyes bright and curious. "We need to know what happened with Declan Parks. Did he ever come back to see the turtle?"

Heat instantly crept up my neck before spreading across my face. I was waiting for this moment, yet I still felt one hundred percent unprepared. Surprisingly, neither of them had bothered me about him until this moment. I couldn't help but wonder if they were waiting for a time when I wouldn't be able to avoid answering them.

"*He did,*" I admitted before picking up my shot to

occupy my hands with something other than answering their questions.

Winter was smiling brightly at me. "Did he come just for the turtle or to see you too?"

I swallowed a mouthful of the mixture of liquor before setting the shot glass back down. *"He didn't just come to see the turtle."*

"I knew it!" Harper exclaimed while slapping her hand on the table. "I told you he wanted to see you too."

I looked back and forth between the two of them, reading their facial expressions. A smile was pulling on my lips and I hated the way my body was betraying me. I couldn't even fight it if I wanted to. Harper's excitement was contagious and Winter was so curious.

"Come on, G. You have to give us more than that." She raised her eyebrows at me. "The suspense is literally killing me."

My phone vibrated on the table beside me and I glanced at it, seeing Declan's name on the screen. Jesus. That man had impeccable timing. It was like the universe buzzed in his ear and let him know we were talking about him.

"Is that him?" Harper questioned me as she tried to look at the screen before it went dark.

I nodded. *"He came back to see the turtle and got my phone number. We ended up running into each other one morning on the beach and went for breakfast."*

Harper's elbows were propped on the table and her

chin was resting on her hands as she waited for me to continue. Winter was leaning against the table, her eyes glued to my hands. I took a deep breath, glancing at my phone as it vibrated with a reminder that I had an unread message.

"Go on and answer him," Winter insisted, pointing at my phone with a wink.

Exhaling deeply, I picked it up and opened my messages. I kept my face as straight as I possibly could, but it was hard when I saw his message.

DECLAN

I miss you.

I quickly typed out a response as warmth spilled into my veins.

GIANA

You just saw me yesterday morning.

After setting my phone back down, I began to sign again. *"He came back again to see Pop-Tart and surprised me by asking me on a date in sign language. He started taking private lessons to learn it."*

"Stop it," Winter said while Harper squealed, "Oh my god," at the same time. Both of their expressions were dreamy and I was waiting for hearts to start floating in their eyes.

"Did you go on a date?" Winter questioned me as my phone went off again.

DECLAN

> That was a lifetime ago. I want to see you again.

I smiled at his message, not caring that Harper and Winter were both watching me with pure curiosity.

GIANA

> I'm out with Winter and Harper right now.

I directed my attention back to my friends. *"We did. We went and got dinner."*

Harper stared at me. "Is that it? Nothing else happened?"

Was I supposed to kiss and tell? They were my best friends, after all. If there was anyone I was going to gossip with, it would be the two of them.

"He kissed me that night, but he wouldn't come in. I don't even know how to explain it or describe it. But it was amazing." I paused, biting the inside of my cheek before blushing again. *"That's not it, though…"*

"I don't even need to read those damn romance novels Wes keeps telling me to read," Harper said as she took another sip of her drink. "There's no way anything in those books can come close to this right now."

I laughed silently, shaking my head at her. Another message came through and I quickly unlocked the screen to read Declan's message.

DECLAN

Come see me after you're done with them.

GIANA

I didn't drive here and I've been drinking.

Winter tapped her hand on the table in front of me to get my attention. I lifted my gaze from my phone, back to her and Harper. They were waiting. I needed to just spill it all now. "What does he want?"

"He wants me to come see him."

Harper's smile reached her eyes. "Girl, why are you still here?"

I tilted my head to the side. *"Because I didn't drive here, remember?"*

Nico drove Harper and I and dropped us off, just like Malakai did with Winter. The boys were at the local Topgolf and left us with the promise of picking us up whenever we were ready to go home.

"Declan took me surfing the other day... Well, he tried to show me the best he could since he's not supposed to be surfing right now because of his shoulder." I paused again. Shit. I was going to tell them. I had to. I was still trying to process everything between the two of us. *"I went back to his place after... and didn't go home until the next morning."*

"Oh my god, G!" Harper clapped her hands together in excitement. "Yes. This is perfect. This is absolutely amazing. How was it?"

Winter cut her eyes at her. "Don't put her on the spot like that. It's kind of rude, especially if she doesn't want to talk about it."

Oh, Winter. She was always the sweetest and if there was one person who never wanted anyone to feel uncomfortable, it was her. She was my best friend since we were kids. Even though some years had passed that we weren't as close when she was in Vermont, she would still always have my back.

"It's fine," I assured her with a smile. Malakai's protectiveness must have really rubbed off on her, even if she and Harper were friends too. *"It was like nothing else I had ever experienced before… and I experienced it a few different times with him while I was at his house. It was mind-blowing."*

My phone went off once again and I checked my newest message from Declan. My heart began to race in my chest and I couldn't fight the stupid grin that was permanently situated on my lips.

DECLAN

> I'll come get you, princess. Let me know when you're ready to leave and I'll be there.

"Girl, you better tell that man to come get you," Harper told me with a look of encouragement. "And I'm sorry if what I said came off as rude. I'm just excited for you because you deserve to be with someone who will treat you like a queen, and let's be real—the damn guy is learning sign language for you."

I looked to Winter who nodded. "She's right. Maybe things are moving fast, but maybe they're moving the way they should be. Life is short, after all, and look at the time Malakai and I lost that we'll never get back."

"You're right," I signed back to the two of them before typing out my response to Declan.

GIANA

Come now. We're at The Lounge.

DECLAN

I'm on my way, princess.

CHAPTER SEVENTEEN
DECLAN

Holding the door open for Giana, she stepped inside my brother's house, looking exactly like she belonged there with me. It wasn't my actual home, but it felt like it was in a sense. There was a part of me that wished we were in California. So I could take her to my own place, to show her my life there. I wanted her in every piece of it.

Stepping up to her, I slid my hand into hers, our fingers intertwining with one another's. She looked up at me, a softness dancing in her eyes with the fire that was burning deeply inside. I watched, entirely mesmerized as she pulled her bottom lip between her teeth and bit down. Her cheeks had a rosy tint from the alcohol and she swayed slightly. If you weren't watching her the way I was, it was a movement that could have easily been missed.

She wasn't drunk, thank God, but she was tipsy. I

would have brought her back with me whether she was drunk or not, but I had plans for her and I wanted her coherent. Taking advantage of her was one thing I would never ever do.

I wanted her sober. I wanted her to wake up in the morning and remember every inch of me that was inside of her. I wanted her to remember every kiss placed on her tender skin.

I wanted her to remember *me.*

Leading her through the house, we didn't stop until we were walking into my bedroom. I flicked on the small bedside lamp so we weren't completely in the dark. My brother was gone for the next few nights, out of town for some medical conference. I was glad to have the house to myself. There wouldn't be any interruptions in my time with Giana.

She walked over to my bed, spinning to face me before she dropped down onto the mattress. Reaching for me with her other hand, she grabbed ahold of me and pulled me down with her. Her dress hiked up her thighs as she scooted up toward the pillows. I followed after her, crawling onto the bed with her.

Hovering over her, her eyes met mine. She quickly glanced at the still open door and back to me. *"Is your brother home?"*

I shook my head at her, my face dipping down to hers as I nipped at her lips. I pulled back so she could read them. "He's gone for a few days. We have the house to ourselves."

She lifted her hands to my chest, gently pushing me away. I sat up and she slid out from under me. Her feet touched the floor and suddenly she was walking back to the bedroom door. I rolled onto my back, staring at her with my eyebrows pinched together.

Giana turned back to me with a smile. *"I'm going to get a drink really quick, if that's okay?"*

My expression relaxed. "Of course. I can get it for you, if you don't feel like getting it."

She shook her head at me. Forming a Y with both of her hands, she held her arms out and thrust her knuckles down with the backs of her hands facing the ceiling. *"Stay."* She winked before disappearing through the doorway.

I wanted her to feel comfortable here, so while I waited, I took off my shirt and tossed it onto the floor. Moving to the pillows, I laid back on the bed with my shorts still on. The last thing I wanted was her to feel like I was expecting something by waiting for her naked. Although, I wasn't opposed to anything she wanted to do.

Lifting my hands, I rested them behind my head and squinted my eyes against the darkness out in the hall. She never turned on a light and I wasn't fully paying attention to the sound of her out there. I didn't hear a door shut, so she was still here, but it shouldn't have been taking her this long to get a water bottle from the fridge.

Suddenly, she appeared back in the doorway. The

oxygen left both my lungs and the room swiftly as my eyes met hers. She was completely naked, her steps full of confidence as she stepped into the room. My breath was trapped in my lungs and my throat bobbed as I swallowed roughly. I watched, completely captivated by her as she sauntered to the end of the bed. The mattress dipped in the slightest bit under her weight as she planted her hands by my feet.

I stared at her, lost in the swirling storm brewing in her ocean blue eyes.

"Get on your knees, princess," I murmured as I simultaneously moved my hands in front of one another before pointing to my chest. "Crawl to me."

Giana moved her hands along the sides of my legs as she lifted her knees onto the mattress. Her back was arched and my eyes traveled across her perfect tits before moving back to her eyes. They were filled with lust, swirling with need as she began to crawl to me. Her legs were on either side of mine, crawling up my body until her face was just above mine.

I reached for her hips, my fingers digging into her flesh. "Don't stop crawling, princess," I told her as her gaze burned through mine. "Don't stop until your hands reach the headboard. Hold on to it and put that pretty pussy in my face."

Her eyes widened. Her lips parted as she was about to mouth something to me, but I lifted my face to hers, silencing her with my mouth. The kiss was heated and hasty as I stole the air from her lungs before abruptly pulling away from her.

My hands were urging her forward. "Sit on my face, Giana. I want to taste you."

"I've never—I don't want to hurt you. I feel like if I sit on you, I'm going to smother you or something."

"I promise you won't," I assured her, grinning. "Although, I wouldn't be opposed to you smothering me with that sweet pussy." My tongue darted out to wet my lips. "Come on, princess. Come take a seat."

She was hesitant, but she obeyed as she moved farther up my body. Her knees were planted on the mattress as she straddled my face. I looked up, watching as she grabbed a hold of the headboard and began to lower herself down to me. My hands moved from her hips to her ass and I gripped her flesh as I urged her pussy to my mouth.

My tongue slid along her and her hips bucked as I swirled it around her clit. Holding her in place, I continued the same movement. I licked and sucked, teasing her clit every time I ran my tongue against her. She tasted so fucking sweet, like nectar. I would never get enough of her.

Of the way she tasted. The way her body writhed against me. The soft sounds, the breathless moans, that escaped her in the throes of ecstasy. She was intoxicating. I wanted to savor every drop—every moment I had with her.

I continued to lap at her pussy before sucking her clit between my lips. She began to grind her center against my face and my chin was soaked with her arousal. Giana cried out as I nibbled on her clit. She was coming undone under my touch just from the way I moved my mouth against her. My grip tightened on her ass cheeks and I held her against my face, breathing in her sweet scent.

My eyes lifted from her stomach, traveling up her body. Her hands were still holding on to the headboard and her lips were parted as every shallow breath escaped her. She was a fucking goddess. So ethereal. So fucking pure. She was the goodness in the world. She was what everyone was looking for—chasing after. And she was all mine.

She just didn't know it yet.

Rolling my tongue over her clit, I applied pressure while repeating the same movements. Swirling, sucking, tasting, teasing. It wasn't long before her thighs tightened around the sides of my face and she cried out. She was a mess of soft breathless moans, and then I heard it. In the midst of her orgasm, as it was wreaking havoc on her body, pulling her deep into the depths of ecstasy—I fucking heard it.

"Declan."

It was so soft, barely audible. Only a whisper she intended on keeping to herself, but I didn't miss it. And Jesus fucking Christ. My heart felt like it was going to burst. Like it was going to detonate inside my chest.

I had never heard a sweeter sound in my entire life.

I continued to roll my tongue against her, drinking every last drop of her until she was blissfully caught in a cloud of euphoria. Giana released the death grip she had on the headboard and began to move down my body. Her hands were already on me, sliding her fingers beneath the waistband of my shorts and boxers.

My eyes met hers. She was lost in a daze and her eyes were heavy as she gave me a slow smile. Lifting my hips, I let her remove the rest of my clothes. I watched her silently as she came back to me, grabbing my cock with one hand as she straddled my lap.

"That's it, princess," I murmured, my voice hoarse as my hands found her hips. "Take what you want from me."

"I want to make you come," she mouthed before moaning softly as she slid down the length of my cock. She took all of it in one fluid movement, sinking in deep until her pelvis met mine. Goddamn. The sight of her on top of me had a ball of heat already spreading across the pit of my stomach.

I swallowed roughly. "Fuck me, princess. Fuck me until I'm filling you with my cum."

She began to lift her hips, her hands planted against my chest. My hands were gripping her hips. Her eyes never once left mine as she began to ride me. I couldn't stop it as my hips began to lift, thrusting into her every time she lowered herself back down onto me.

We were caught in the moment, meeting each other in the middle as she fucked me and I fucked her back. I was forever gone for her. My fingers dug into her skin as I began to take over, lifting her before dropping her back down onto my length. I was filling her deeply with every thrust. My heart was beating to its own erratic melody in my chest.

But Giana and those goddamn ocean blue eyes.

She never once tore her gaze away from mine. Not as her body began to shake. As her legs gripped the sides of my hips, her lips parted and a cry escaped her as another orgasm began to build within her. I tried to fight my own, but I couldn't. She clenched around me as she fell over the edge, shattering into a million pieces. My balls constricted and my own orgasm spread through my body like wildfire.

It was consuming. Dangerous. And fucking beautiful.

Her lips were parted as soft moans escaped her. She kept riding me, riding out the waves of both of our orgasms as I lost myself inside her. I spilled myself into her, filling her with my cum. I was so deep inside her and I never wanted any of this to end.

Giana Cirone had already pierced through my heart, I just didn't know how deeply until that moment.

That breathtaking, beautiful moment as she stared down at me like I had filled the ocean with the very water that kept it alive. She was so terribly wrong.

She was the one that kept it alive... not me.

CHAPTER EIGHTEEN
GIANA

Lifting my arms above my head, I stretched out my sore limbs and slowly rolled over to face Declan. His warmth was radiating from his body and I watched the way his chest rose and fell with every gentle breath he took. It should have felt weird, waking up in someone else's bed, but it didn't. There was something about him that brought peace to my soul. He made me feel comforted in ways I had never felt before. I reveled in the way he made me feel.

Safe.

My eyes traveled across his features. His face was so relaxed. Angelic, if you will. There wasn't a touch of concern, yet I wasn't quite sure I had witnessed that in him since the day he brought Pop-Tart to the rehabilitation center. He was always at ease, but in his sleep, there was an innocence about him. I couldn't tear my eyes from him even if I wanted to.

"I can feel you watching me, princess." His lips barely moved, but I could still make out the words. His eyes were still closed as he reached out for me. I rolled in the opposite direction, just as his arm snaked around my waist and he pulled me flush against him. My back was pressed against his chest, enveloped in his warmth.

A smile crept onto my lips and I scooted as close as I could get to him, relaxing in his arms. He buried his face in my hair before moving to my neck. His mouth was soft against my skin, tender and gentle as he peppered kisses against my flesh. He nuzzled his face against me, breathing in deeply.

I wasn't sure how long we stayed like that, but the sun was shining brightly through his bedroom window when we both finally climbed out of bed. Declan bent over to collect our clothes and I studied him. The way his body moved. His skin stretched across his taut muscles. He was handcrafted by the ocean gods. How did I end up catching the attention of someone like him?

He tossed my panties to me and one of his t-shirts and nothing else. I lifted an eyebrow at him and he simply winked. Heat crept across my cheeks. I ducked my head, creating a curtain around my face with my hair before slipping on his shirt. After I dressed, I glanced at Declan who was pulling on a pair of shorts.

"Are you hungry?" he asked me.

My stomach growled in response and he smiled as I nodded. *"Starving."*

His smile transformed into a smirk and mischief danced in his golden brown irises. "Me too. But I'll settle for food right now instead."

My mouth instantly went dry as Declan walked past me, exiting his bedroom without another word. I was momentarily frozen in place before I snapped out of it. I'd never experienced someone like him before... and I wasn't sure I wanted to experience this with anyone but him. Turning on my heel, I quickly followed him out through the house and found him in the kitchen pulling things from the fridge.

He motioned for me to sit down at the island. I watched him as he poured me a glass of orange juice and set it down in front of me. He pulled eggs from the refrigerator, along with some peppers and onions that were already diced. Declan moved around the kitchen like he knew exactly what he was doing. I was mesmerized, watching him complete the simple task of making eggs with ease.

Living on my own, I had to learn how to cook, but it wasn't something I would say I was good at. I couldn't make pancakes without burning them. If it came with instructions and I followed them, I could usually make an edible meal. Except for pancakes, of course. I had managed thus far, but it was always nice when someone else cooked. It wasn't my strong suit.

Declan set a plate in front of me that was equipped with quite possibly the best eggs someone had ever made me, along with two slices of buttered toast. He watched me for a moment with hopeful eyes as I took a bite. It tasted even better than it looked.

"How is it?"

I swallowed and took a sip of my juice. *"Delicious. Better than anything I could have made."*

He smiled while he stood across from me with his own plate. He could have taken the seat beside me, but it would have made it a little more difficult for us to talk. Instead, he made sure he was in front of me. "Are you a bad cook?"

A shy smile danced across my lips and I shrugged. *"I don't know about bad, but I wouldn't say good."*

"Well, it's a good thing I'm a pretty decent cook then," he replied with a wink. "I'll cook for you any chance I get."

Something about his words struck a chord in my heart. The consideration he had for others had my chest constricting. It was the little things he did, the ones that would normally go unnoticed, except they didn't. Not to me. I noticed it all.

Living the majority of my life in silence gave me the time to appreciate what was going on around me. I was able to observe and study without the outside noise. And Declan Parks was by far my most favorite subject.

We both fell into our own thoughts as we enjoyed the meal he made. I would gladly let him make me food anytime he wanted to. My stomach was full and he looked pleased as he took my empty plate and rinsed it off. He placed the dirty dishes in the dishwasher before turning back around to face me. I took another sip of my orange juice, still watching him as his gaze collided with mine.

"Let's do something today." He stepped back over to the island and planted his hands on the countertop. "Do you want to go to the beach? It's supposed to be beautiful out today."

I nodded. *"That sounds perfect."* I paused for a moment, as I realized I had nothing with me but the clothes I wore last night. *"I need to go back to my house to get a bathing suit and stuff, though."*

His eyes were shining as he looked at me. They always had a way of glimmering when he stared into mine. "I'll take you, princess. Maybe you can pack a bag and come stay with me for another day or two?"

My stomach did a somersault. *"I'd like that."*

"So would I." He grinned. "Did you want to call your friends and see if they wanted to meet us at the beach?"

I tilted my head to the side as curiosity mixed with the adrenaline rushing through me. *"Are you sure?"* He didn't know any of them, but the thought didn't seem to bother him in the slightest.

"If they're important people in your life, I'd like to meet them if you want me to."

"If I invite Harper, my brother will most likely come with her if he doesn't have any hockey stuff going on."

Declan didn't seem fazed. "Perfect. I was hoping I'd get the chance to meet him soon."

Now he really had me curious. *"Why?"*

"So I can make sure he knows I have no intention of ever breaking your heart."

The air left my lungs in a rush. I was yet again frozen in place. Declan moved away from the counter as if he didn't just speak those words out loud. They swirled around in my head, nestling deep within the crevices of my mind. Those words were imprinted in every synapse, effectively altering my brain chemistry.

I have no intention of ever breaking your heart.

What could he possibly intend on doing with it then?

"Come on, princess," he said as he rounded the island and reached for me. "Let's get ready to go."

I didn't protest and I didn't question him as I slid my hand into his. He led me back into his bedroom where I didn't bother to slip out of his t-shirt. The bottom hem brushed against my legs mid-thigh and it covered up enough that I wasn't going to change back into my dress from last night. Declan had a spare tooth-brush for me in his bathroom and after I used it, he slid it into the holder where his was.

We headed out to his Jeep and Declan, being the perfect gentleman that he is, held the door open for me and closed it after I climbed inside. The butterflies in my stomach refused to tire of the endless fluttering of their wings. He wasn't going out of his way to do the things he did for me. He just did them because he wanted to. Because it all felt so goddamn natural.

Declan was like a continuous drip of heroin in my veins.

And I was hopelessly addicted.

I pulled out my phone as he pulled his car onto the street and opened up the group chat between Winter, Harper, and me. I asked both of them if they wanted to meet us at the beach for the day. Winter was the first to reply, saying to tell her where and when. She didn't specify if Malakai was coming or not, but knowing him, he went wherever Winter went.

Harper's message came in next, saying she and Nico would both be there. I knew my brother well enough to know he wouldn't pass up the opportunity to finally meet Declan. I just hoped he wouldn't try to scare him off too much. Nico was a little protective, to say the least.

Declan stopped at a stop sign and glanced over at me with an eyebrow raised in question.

"Harper and Winter both said yes and they would meet us there." I let out a shaky breath. *"My brother's coming too, and maybe Malakai, Winter's boyfriend."*

He smiled brightly as he slid his hand to my bare thigh. "Don't be nervous, princess," he assured me. His palm was warm on my skin and he moved his thumb across my flesh as he held on to my leg. "I'm not afraid of your brother. There isn't anything or anyone that could possibly chase me away from you."

I returned his smile and nodded. His hand didn't leave my thigh as he directed his attention back to the road and began driving again. I hoped he was right because I wasn't sure how I would take it if he changed his mind about all of this.

I was already sinking deep into the depths of him.

The surface no longer existed.

I was entirely lost in the ocean of Declan Parks.

CHAPTER NINETEEN
GIANA

D eclan pulled his Jeep into the small parking lot by the public beach access area. My brother's car was already in one of the spots with Malakai's parked next to his. Declan parked next to the two of them and when we got out, he refused to let me help him unload or carry any of the stuff we brought along. I followed after him, pulling my sunglasses down over my face to block out the bright sunlight.

Declan had two chairs on his back, his surfboard tucked under his good arm, and a bag with towels hoisted over the other shoulder. A smile pulled on my lips and I shook my head at his back as I watched him trudge through the soft white sand. The ocean breeze drifted across the shore, blowing my hair around my face.

There were only a few other groups of people on the

beach and I caught sight of Harper's bright blonde hair as she stood beside Winter, Nico, and Malakai. Malakai was shoving the end of an umbrella into the sand as Nico unfolded their chairs and set them up. Harper and Winter were both standing off to the side, lost in conversation. And there was Wes, fumbling with an E-Z Up.

Both of the girls' heads whipped in our direction as they saw Declan and I heading toward them. Winter raised her hand to wave us over and I smiled at the sight of them. We've had our girls' nights and I've hung out with my brother a few times, but with everyone's busy schedules, it was hard for all of us to get together like this. It felt like it had been a century since we all hung out.

Declan's footsteps slowed and I walked up beside him. He glanced over at me with a hint of worry in his expression. His eyes were covered by his sunglasses and I couldn't see what was going on inside of them.

"I'm never nervous," he admitted to me. "But I'd be lying if I said I wasn't right now."

I shook my head at him. *"Don't be. There isn't a single thing not to love about you."* My eyes widened as I tried to backtrack. *"What I mean is, they'll love you."*

His eyebrows lifted very subtly and his mouth twitched, but he didn't say anything else. I turned my head away from him as heat crept up my neck and rapidly spread across my cheeks. It wasn't from the sun that was beating down on us either. It was my damn word vomit.

All five of them turned to look at us as we walked over and I let the embarrassment vanish. My brother jogged over, wrapping his arm around the tops of my shoulders as he pulled me against his sweaty body. I silently laughed and pushed him away while scrunching my nose in disgust.

He laughed at me, stumbling in the sand before turning to Declan. "Let me help you with that." His lips moved as he reached out for Declan's board. "I'm Nico," he held his hand out to him.

Declan took it without hesitation and shook it. "I'm Declan." He let Nico take his surfboard from him. "Thanks, man."

Nico nodded and propped it in the sand as Declan dropped our bag down by the umbrella before helping Wes with the E-Z Up. Both of the girls went over to him and introduced themselves. Malakai simply nodded at him and his lips barely moved as he told him his name while dropping down onto one of the chairs. I imagined he probably mumbled the words in annoyance. Malakai could never be bothered by anyone but Winter and maybe my brother.

I smiled at my friends and helped Declan with our two chairs. I tucked them under the E-Z Up as Wes introduced himself to him. It wasn't surprising seeing him here. Wes and my brother were stuck together like glue. Sometimes, I felt bad for Harper, but she didn't seem to mind that they were together all the time. A part of me felt bad for Wes that he always seemed to be the third—or fifth—or seventh wheel, in this case.

He wasn't shy with women and frequently had one he was talking to, but it was never serious. I had never actually seen him in a relationship in the past few years that I knew him.

Wes grabbed a football and tossed it into the air. "You guys wanna play a game?"

Malakai rolled his eyes in response and reached for Winter, before pulling her onto his lap. Her head tipped back, her face lighting up as she laughed and settled against him. I couldn't read their lips as they fell into a quiet conversation together. I felt like I was invading an intimate moment between the two of them.

I looked back around the circle of friends. Declan was watching me for a moment before he glanced over at Wes.

"I'm actually going to hop in the water quickly and then I'll be down to play."

Wes nodded and Nico and Harper agreed. With how hot it already was, everyone was ready to get into the water. The three of them headed toward the ocean and I grabbed the sunscreen from the bag Declan carried out here. I squirted some into my hands and bent down as I began to rub the lotion into my legs. After my skin was covered, I slowly stood back upright.

Declan's eyes were on mine. I still couldn't see them through his sunglasses, but I didn't need to in order to see the fire burning in his gaze. I could feel the heat rolling off his body in waves. I didn't break eye contact with him as I rubbed the lotion over the rest of my body and closed the distance between us as I held it out to him.

He was silent as he took the bottle from me and I slowly turned around, pulling my hair away from the nape of my neck. I waited as I stared out at the waves breaking against the shore. A few breaths later, I felt Declan's fingertips graze the skin on my shoulders. His touch was light and tender, a warning he was behind me. He did it so he wouldn't frighten me.

I smiled as his fingers didn't leave my shoulder. His other hand flattened against the top of my back and he began to work the sunscreen into my skin. My eyelids fluttered shut and I leaned against his touch. I never wanted him to stop touching me, but he did. He circled around, making sure he covered every inch before moving his hands away from me.

Taking off my sunglasses, I dropped them down into our bag. I glanced over my shoulder at him and nodded toward the ocean. He set his sunglasses down with mine. A smile coasted across his lips and he left his board behind as he fell into step beside me. It was a short distance to the water. We had only taken a few strides before I felt his hand slide against mine. I glanced over at him, a little taken aback by the action. Declan simply smiled at me as he laced his fingers through mine and we stepped into the ocean together.

The water was cooler than the water in the Gulf, but it was still warm from the hot summer sun. It slid past my ankles and the two of us kept moving forward, walking into the deeper waters of the ocean. I caught my brother's eye as he and Harper were swimming out past where the waves were breaking. His gaze slid down to Declan's hand still wrapped around mine.

We were closing in on where they were and Declan released my hand as he dove through the water. I watched him, in awe of the way his muscles moved as he extended his hands above his head and slid through the surface of the ocean. You wouldn't think he had done any damage to his shoulder with the way he swam. He was an extremely strong swimmer.

His head popped back up through the surface and he bobbed in the water about six feet away from me. A smile pulled on his lips as he began to swim toward me. I stepped deeper into the water as it was moving farther up my body. It was just above my breasts and I bent my knees as I dropped down, slipping under the water.

Straightening my body, I floated to the surface on my back. I didn't move my limbs and let the salt water carry me as the waves shifted me gently. My ears were beneath the water. I was used to the silence of the world around me, but there was something comforting about the silence of the ocean. Beneath the surface, it was peaceful and quiet. I couldn't remember what the ocean really sounded like, but I knew its silence well.

It wrapped itself around me, warm and comforting.

The water felt like silk against my skin. It was like a massive blanket enveloping me, rocking me with the gentleness of a mother with a child. The ocean was known to be angry and vicious, yet she was also kind and tender. As long as you respected her, she treated you with the same kindness.

Declan's palms were soft against my flesh as he slid one hand under my upper back and the other beneath my thighs. My eyelids lifted and I turned my head to see him as he pulled me into his arms. The water was lapping against his chest and he pulled me firmly against him as I lifted my upper body from the water.

"What are you doing?" I mouthed to him. With the amount of time we had been spending together, he was getting better at reading lips.

He tilted his head to the side. "Do you want me to let you go, princess?" A smile pulled on his lips. "Do you not want anyone to see us like this?"

My throat bobbed as I swallowed roughly. I mulled over his words for a moment while pulling my bottom lip between my teeth. This was different for me. In a way, I was like Wes. I knew all eyes were on the two of us right now because I had never brought a guy around everyone. No one was ever serious enough to introduce to my friends or family.

Is that what we were?

Were we something serious?

I shook my head at him. *"No."* I paused for a

moment as I wrapped my arms around the back of his neck. *"Don't let me go, Declan."*

Instead of signing the letters of his name, I signed the letter *D* and held it to my heart.

"What was that?" he questioned me as his eyes widened in surprise.

I swallowed roughly. *"It's the way I sign your name… you know, so I don't have to sign the letters every time."*

His golden brown eyes shimmered under the sun hanging in the sky above us as emotion swirled within his irises. "I'll never let you go," he assured me as he pressed his forehead against mine. He pulled the two of us deeper into the water until neither of our feet could touch the bottom.

He didn't break his promise. He didn't let me go. Not until he finally walked us back to the beach, and only then did he let my feet touch the sand. But his hand still found mine as we walked back to everyone waiting for us on the beach.

I didn't mean just in the ocean…

I didn't want him to ever let me go.

CHAPTER TWENTY
DECLAN

J umping up in the air, I caught the football Malakai hurled at me. I knew he was a professional golfer, but he surprised me with the strength of his throw. A part of me was wondering if he did it intentionally. He didn't want to play with us, but we needed a fourth player. Nico and Wes declared themselves as the dream team, so that left me with this moody, broody guy instead.

I began to run through the sand, ducking past Wes as he dove at me. Malakai was deliberately slow as he moved away from Nico, yet he effortlessly caught the ball when I threw it back to him. He glanced at Nico and quickly shifted away from him. He stepped closer to the line drawn in the sand for a touchdown and at the last minute, he threw it back to me.

Wes tackled me, effectively knocking the ball free from my grip. I rolled across the rough surface with a twinge of annoyance nipping at my nerves. Wes laughed loudly and tossed the football to Nico. He held his hand out to me. "Sorry about that, man," he said with a chuckle as he helped me to my feet. "Sometimes I play a little too aggressively. Blame it on the ice hockey."

"I know what the three of you are up to," I told him matter-of-factly. "This is like a hazing in a way. You're all protective of Giana, which I don't blame you for at all. I can take it."

Wes winked. "Smart one, aren't you?"

"Well, I'm not stupid." I paused for a moment, nodding my head at my teammate. "What's his deal, though? He's, like, self-sabotaging by playing against me while he's on my team."

"Kai?" Wes said as he glanced over at my teammate who was walking over to Winter instead of continuing the game. "He's a peculiar guy. Unless you're his girl-friend, you're relatively insignificant in his life."

I watched as he dropped down onto the chair next to her. He only had eyes for her. Winter glanced over at him with a soft smile, her hand instinctively reaching out for him. "I can see that." There was a part of me that realized that was what I wanted. I wanted what they had... and I couldn't imagine it with anyone other than Giana.

Wes walked back over to where the girls were. My gaze followed him for a moment before landing on Giana. She was sitting on a chair and Harper was on a blanket by her feet. The two of them were deep in conversation, signing to one another. A smile danced across my lips as I watched them. I studied the side of Giana's face, my eyes trailing over the perfect curves of her body as my gaze moved down farther.

She was absolutely breathtaking. The most beautiful thing to ever grace my vision.

"She's pretty fucking special, isn't she?" Nico questioned me as he stepped up behind me. I didn't even hear him walking through the powder-like sand. I slowly turned around to face him. He was staring at his sister before directing his attention to me. "Mind if we have a word?"

"Not at all." I shook my head, knowing this was coming. And I was fully prepared for this talk.

Nico motioned for me to walk with him and we headed down to the water. I stared out at the horizon, watching the way the ocean disappeared where it met the sky. It was as if it went on forever and ever.

"Tell me about yourself, Declan."

I turned to face Nico. "There's not much to tell. I grew up on the West Coast in Malibu. Grew up surfing and went professional when I was in my late teens. Haven't looked back since."

Nico nodded, but he already knew most of this. He wasn't an idiot. I didn't need him to tell me he did whatever internet research he could to find out anything about me. It wasn't like he would have had to look too hard. Although, none of it was anything about my personal life.

"What brings you to Orchid City?"

I pointed to my left shoulder. "At a tournament in Oahu, I lost my balance and dislocated my shoulder. I decided to come stay with my brother and do all of my rehab here with his friend who is a physical therapist."

"Ah, yes. Your brother, Adrian. He's a damn good doctor. We're lucky to have him on the team."

"He is," I agreed, pausing for a moment. "You didn't question him about me at all?"

Nico shook his head and smiled. "I didn't want someone else's thoughts on you. I wanted to meet you myself to be able to form my own opinion on you."

"I like that," I told him, smiling back. We fell into a moment of silence that stretched between us before Nico spoke again.

"I'll be honest, I know enough about your professional career. It's impressive as hell." He turned to face me completely in a nonconfrontational manner. "I want to know your intentions with my sister. Giana is all I have besides Harper and those other fuckers over there. I'm not here to threaten you, but I need to know where this is going because the last thing I'm going to do is stand by and wait for my sister to get hurt."

I stared back at him and spoke with no hesitation. "I have no intention of breaking your sister's heart. The last thing I would ever want to do is hurt her."

"She likes you, Declan. A lot." He let out a ragged

breath. "If you aren't serious about this between you and her, you need to let her go now. I know my sister. I've never seen her like this with anyone before, and that's exactly how I know she's falling for you—if she hasn't already. Her feelings for you are deep. You need to end it now if the feelings aren't mutual."

"I'm all in, Nico." I paused for a moment, collecting my thoughts before I rambled a bunch of nonsense and poured all of my feelings for her to him. "Giana is the most amazing person I've ever met. She has completely captivated me. I have no intentions of ever breaking her heart, because I am in deeper than I even imagined to be possible. I'm all in with her. I just haven't exactly told her yet."

Nico studied me. "I'm glad to hear that. I just have one more question." He turned his head to look back up to where Giana was sitting before looking back to me. "I imagine when your shoulder is healed, you will be going back to the West Coast."

There it was. I had a feeling this would be coming from him. And it was something that had been lingering in the back of my mind, the farther Giana pulled me into her swell.

I let out a soft breath and nodded. "That was the plan. I was only supposed to be staying here until my shoulder was healed and I could go back to finish some of the tournaments I'm already registered for."

"And what happens with Giana then? Will you ask her to go with you or will you leave her behind?"

I swallowed roughly, shaking my head. "I've been trying to not think about it. She has an entire life built here. The last thing I want to do is uproot her. I could travel back and forth." I stopped and let out a sigh as my shoulders hung heavily in defeat. "I haven't figured it out."

Nico frowned slightly as he stared at me, but a knowing look took over his expression. "I get it. These damn professional sports… it's what we've worked so hard for our entire lives, but priorities can change so easily when the heart gets involved."

I was appreciative of his comment, of him letting me into his own thoughts for a moment. He played hockey professionally. There were many days and nights spent on the road, flying around the country for other games.

"Is it hard on Harper when you have to travel?"

Nico shook his head. "Not anymore. It was at first, but she's grown used to the lifestyle. We make it work and she does travel with me sometimes."

"I'm glad the two of you are able to make it work."

"Me too," he said softly and nodded. "Although, we're not living on two opposite sides of the country. If things are really getting this serious between you and my sister, I think it's a conversation worth having sooner than rather later. She needs to know what she's getting into, especially if you plan on going back and staying there."

He was right. I turned back to look at Giana who was watching the two of us. I smiled at her and her lips stretched into a warm smile as she lifted her hand to wave me over.

"I'm sure it's killing her, not knowing what we're talking about right now." Nico chuckled as he turned to face the group. "Although, I'm sure she knows I'm questioning you on your intentions."

"She's definitely going to be asking me about it later."

Nico looked back at me once more. "I like you, Declan. Don't fuck this up and don't break my sister's fucking heart. I have no problem breaking every bone in your body if I have to."

I smiled back at him and extended my hand to his. "I give you permission to do so if I do, but I can assure you that won't be necessary."

He took my hand and shook it. "I can deal with that."

We released one another's hands and began to walk back up the beach toward everyone. Giana's gaze held mine and she smiled up at me as I stopped in front of her. Her ocean blue eyes explored mine with so many questions, but there was more lingering in her irises. She looked at me the way I loved. The way I wanted her to always look at me.

I wouldn't be breaking her heart, so I needed to find a way to make this work. There had to be a solution to this and if it came down to choosing between Giana and surfing, my heart had already made its decision.

It would be Giana.

CHAPTER TWENTY-ONE
GIANA

The hospital was calm when I got to work on Monday morning. Everyone was already busy with their work and Miranda gave me a quick rundown of some things that needed to be done with the animals in the facility. I stopped by my lab first to check my emails from over the weekend.

There was one from my boss, Richard. He oversaw the day-to-day operations in the facility and was the person we had to get things approved by. It wasn't often he was around, but every now and then, he and his team stopped by to make sure things were running smoothly. I had forgotten I had asked him about Declan volunteering until I saw Richard's response.

My eyes scanned the computer screen, reading over his approval. He thought it would be beneficial to have someone like Declan volunteer. Richard must have done his research and realized Declan was an exceptional surfer who had quite the loyal following. It could be good for the facility to gain some publicity with the help of Declan.

I couldn't help but frown. We could use any help we could get here, but in a way it didn't feel right. It was like Declan's help was only wanted because of who he was, because of his status. I knew Richard wanted what the rest of us did here. For others to care about the ocean and its inhabitants the same way we did.

Maybe any publicity wouldn't be a bad thing. It felt cheap and dirty, but the facility could benefit from it. I was conflicted, but we needed Declan. Not only were we experiencing a shortage in employees, but we were also taking a bit of a financial hit. I needed to stop thinking about it in a negative manner and take it as a way that we could possibly generate more money to keep the facility afloat. State and government grants only went so far.

I typed out a quick response to my boss, thanking him and telling him I'd be in touch after I spoke with Declan about it. After responding to a few other emails, I abandoned my desk and set out through the facility to check off the tasks on my list. My last stop was the turtle building. They needed to get their morning medicine, a quick evaluation, and they all needed to be fed.

Thankfully, we hadn't had any new turtles come in within the past week, so there was only one that was left in quarantine still. We kept them there for ten days, just to make sure they didn't have any illnesses that could be passed on to any of the other turtles. Pop-Tart had passed her quarantine date, but we were still keeping her in a separate pool until her flipper was completely healed.

I made my rounds, making sure each turtle got the appropriate medication and food for the day. Pop-Tart was last on my list. She was the one who had worked her way into my heart. I had an emotional attachment to her. I always made sure to stop by every morning when I arrived and I checked in on her before I left. Sometimes, I spent my lunch eating here, sitting in silence with an animal that couldn't communicate with me.

But in her own way, she did. It was the nonverbal kind. It was something I had grown so accustomed to over the years. It made a connection deeper and having that with a wild animal was something I could never explain to someone who hadn't experienced it themselves.

Pop-Tart looked up at me with her soft and kind marble eyes. There was a gentleness to her, a tenderness. Even though physical contact was minimal, she always watched me. Not with fright, but more so with curiosity. I injected her meds into the body of a dead crab. Dropping it into the water, she hesitated momentarily before grabbing it.

When I first learned about loggerheads and began to study them, it surprised me to find out that hatchlings were omnivores, but the adults were carnivores. We made sure we had a balanced diet tailored to each turtle. Pop-Tart seemed to favor the crabs and conchs we had been feeding her.

I dropped a few more things into her pool and leaned against the side of it, watching as she moved around the water. She glided with ease. Her leg had been getting stronger and stronger each day. Our time with her was growing shorter. It wouldn't be long before she would be released back into her natural habitat in the wild. As much as I loved having her here, I knew that was where she belonged.

It was never easy releasing them back into the ocean. Not when you had an emotional attachment.

We were able to track the ones we tagged before rereleasing, but there were no plans of tagging Pop-Tart. I would have no idea about her life after she was returned to the Atlantic.

Pulling out my phone, I opened my messages and tapped on Declan's name. He hadn't seen Pop-Tart in a few days and when he last did, she wasn't swimming like she was today. I took a quick video and sent it to him before tucking my phone back in my back pocket. A smile touched my lips as I watched Pop-Tart stop in front of me. Her eyes met mine before slowly moving to look past me.

I slowly turned around to see what she was looking at. My breathing hitched and my heart skipped a beat when my gaze collided with Declan's. My eyes widened in surprise as I found him standing behind me. I wasn't expecting him here. We talked last night, but he never mentioned anything about stopping by.

"She looks good." Declan smiled as he nodded his head in Pop-Tart's direction. "Even better than she did in the video you just sent me."

Heat crept up my neck and I shifted my weight nervously on my feet. *"She's healing really well,"* I signed to him while moving my lips to the words to help him better understand what I was saying. *"What are you doing here?"*

"I wanted to come see you." He smiled with his eyes. "And Pop-Tart too."

My eyes slowly examined his. *"I'm glad you stopped by,"* I admitted to him. It wasn't a lie in the slightest bit. I found myself wanting to be around him more and more.

"Me too," he said as he reached up to brush a stray hair from my face that had broken free from my braid. "Tell me about her. What's going on with her now?"

"We're just waiting on her flipper to be fully healed now. The stitches will probably be removed later this week and then she'll be with us for a little longer, just to make sure every-thing healed completely and properly." I paused momen-tarily as a frown tugged my lips downward. *"After she's rehabilitated, we'll release her back into the ocean."*

Declan stared at me for a few moments. "You don't want to release her, do you?"

"I just worry," I explained with a shrug as I tried to hide my emotions. *"I don't know what will happen to her*

once she's back out there. I've grown relatively attached to her, but I know the ocean is where she belongs. It wouldn't be fair to keep her in captivity just because I'm afraid of nature taking its course."

Declan's eyebrows pinched together as he tried to keep up with the movement of my hands and lips. Judging on the way his expression softened and he nodded, he was able to piece together pieces of what I said to him.

"It's completely out of your control, but you already know that," he told me as he ran a hand through his tousled hair. "Mother Nature is a force of her own. Life is completely unpredictable. All we can do is hope for the best, and just know you did everything in your power to keep Pop-Tart safe. You saved her life. That in itself is something to be proud of."

"I was doing what I'm supposed to do."

Declan shook his head at me. "No. You did what most people aren't able to do. You *saved* her. You gave her a second chance at life." He closed the space between us, both of his hands cupping my cheeks as he leaned his face down to mine. "When will you realize how amazing you are?"

Even though I couldn't hear his words, I could still feel them. The weight and the warmth of them as they slithered up my spine. His question wasn't a real question, but it was permanently imprinted in my mind. He thought I was amazing, and he looked at me like I created the entire universe with my two hands.

"Are you busy this evening?"

I raised a curious eyebrow at him and shook my head.

Declan smiled. "What time do you get done with work?"

"Probably around five or six."

"Perfect." His eyes were burning holes through mine. "Save some time for me afterward, princess."

"What did you have in mind?"

A chuckle vibrated in Declan's chest and I could feel it in my own. He shook his head. "It's a surprise."

"You and your surprises," I mouthed after sighing dramatically.

"You love it," he said just before his lips met mine. They were deliberately slow as he took his time kissing me. His tongue was like silk against mine, dancing, tasting, teasing. He breathed me in and I wholly surrendered myself to him.

His surprises weren't the only thing I loved...

CHAPTER TWENTY-TWO
DECLAN

"What are we doing at the marina?" Giana asked me with her hands as a wave of confusion passed through her expression. We were still in my car and I had just turned off the engine when she abruptly turned to me in question.

I told her nothing about the evening I had planned before coming here. I wanted to surprise her. I loved the excitement and the way her face lit up when the realization dawned on her. What I loved even more was when I was able to surprise her without her knowing it was coming. Like stopping by to see her when she wasn't expecting me.

A twinge of sadness tickled the synapses in my brain. I wouldn't be able to do things like this after I went back to the other side of the country. I wouldn't be able to stop by and see her whenever I wanted. I would be fucking thousands of miles away from her.

I pushed the thoughts away from my mind. I couldn't entertain them now.

I drew my attention back to Giana and those ocean blue eyes of hers. "I guess you'll just have to come with me to find out."

Her lips parted as if she was going to say something, but instead she clamped them shut. She reached for the door, getting out before I had the chance to help her. A frustrated sigh escaped me and I quickly climbed out of the Jeep. Giana met me around the back of it. I pulled open the door to the trunk and Giana peered in.

Inside, there was a thermal bag that kept food warm. A paisley fabric design kept the contents inside hidden, not even giving away the fact that there was food inside. I did have another bag that had a few things in it. Giana tried to look in it, but I quickly grabbed it and moved it out of her sight. Closing the trunk, I held on to both of the bags and shook my head at Giana as she offered to take one of them.

"I don't trust you not to look," I told her with a smile.

"You're not going to tell me anything, are you?"

I shook my head at her. "I've never been one to ruin a surprise."

Giana drew in a deep breath before letting out an exasperated, wholly defeated sigh. I held my free hand out to her and she didn't hesitate. She slid her palm against mine, our fingers lacing together. Giana fell into step beside me as I led her down the dock. We reached a boat near the end and stopped by it.

Gabriel came up the steps from underneath the deck. His face lit up as he saw the two of us. "Hey, Dec. You're right on time." He looked over at Giana with a smile. "You must be Giana. I'm Gabriel. I've heard a lot about you."

She smiled at him. *"It's nice to meet you too,"* she mouthed and signed for me to translate, but I didn't bother. Her brow furrowed as she looked between the two of us and settled her gaze on mine. *"Is he taking us out on his boat?"*

Gabriel shook his head. "No. I'm afraid I can't join the two of you tonight. But Declan here is a pretty good driver, so I think you'll be in good hands out there with him."

Giana looked directly at me with her eyes wide, but I simply winked at her as I stepped onto the boat. Setting down the two bags, I held my hand out to her and helped her on board. Gabriel went over a few things with me, but he knew I was more than capable. Growing up on the ocean had its perks that included learning how to operate and drive a boat at a young age.

Gabriel waited until the engine was running and everything looked good before he hopped off onto the dock. He looked between Giana and me. "The two of you have a good night now," he spoke out loud while simultaneously signing the words. "I'll see you tomorrow, Dec. Just bring the keys along with you then."

I nodded at him and waved goodbye as I put the boat in reverse and began to back it out of its respective spot. Gabriel didn't wait to see us off and he disappeared from our view just as I turned the boat around. Giana took a seat in front of me and glanced back at me once more with a smile as I put the boat in drive and eased it away from the dock.

As we moved farther away from the marina and into the open waters, I gave it more gas. We were heading in the direction of the horizon. I wanted to take Giana to where the ocean met the sky. That's what it felt like with her. Like we were forever suspended within that sacred space.

We drove about a mile offshore before I turned off the engine and let the boat float. The waters were calm since there were no impending storms in the forecast. It was a beautiful, peaceful evening—exactly what I wanted with her.

Giana watched me with curiosity as I came around to the front of the boat. I grabbed the two bags and lifted them up to where she was sitting. Inside the uninsulated bag was silverware, plates, and napkins, along with some snacks and a bottle of champagne. Two reusable cups were also inside. I moved to the heated bag and unzipped it before pulling out a glass container.

Her eyes lit up as I opened the container and the

smell of the pasta dish drifted around us, carried by the steam. *"Did you make this?"*

I suddenly felt shy in front of her. I smiled sheepishly and nodded. "I figured pasta was safe. I don't know of anyone who doesn't like pasta."

Emotion welled in her eyes. *"It's perfect."*

"You're perfect."

The words tumbled from my lips and I didn't bother taking them back. They were the truth and she deserved nothing less than that. I fell silent and Giana's eyes tracked my movements as I piled some food onto her plate and handed it to her. She thanked me silently and waited until I had my food before digging in. I watched as she speared her pasta with her fork. Her lips parted and she pushed it into her mouth. Her eyelids fluttered shut as she savored the flavor. I felt like I won the goddamn lottery.

There wasn't a single thing wrong with the night. The weather was amazing. Being on the East Coast, this side of the country was better for sunrises than it was for sunsets. I also didn't want to have Gabriel's boat out here late, just in case anything were to happen. The two of us were quiet as we finished and I took Giana's empty plate and cutlery before tossing it all into the bag.

"That was amazing," she signed to me with a soft smile. *"Thank you for this, Declan."*

"I'm not finished yet." I pulled out a smaller insulated bag and opened it up, showing her the two slices of cheesecake inside. "Are you hungry for dessert?"

She stared at me for a moment with an unidentifiable look in her eye. Her tongue slipped out of her mouth as she wet her lips. *"I'm hungry for something."*

A chuckle vibrated in my throat. My cock was listening and it throbbed in my pants. "That can wait. Let me feed you first."

The fire in her eyes burned brightly as she watched me. Her slender throat bobbed and she pulled her bottom lip between her teeth as I scooted closer to her. Inhaling deeply, the smell of her floral perfume invaded my senses. She was everywhere, consuming me. There was nothing I could do to stop this from happening now and I wouldn't have tried if I could.

My future never felt as uncertain as it did at that moment. I thought I had life figured out before I met Giana Cirone. Things were simple and uncomplicated. I had my career and surfing was the only thing I needed. If only things were that simple now… But everything had changed—all because of her. I had backed myself into a corner, but it was my turn to make a move. I just wasn't sure what I was supposed to do.

Popping off the lid of the container, I grabbed an unused fork and slid it through the thick cheesecake. Giana's eyes were glued to my face, studying me as I lifted the piece into the air. My gaze met hers and the air between us was a storm of electricity. Her jaw dropped as she opened her mouth and I slid the fork in between her lips. She wrapped them around the utensil as I slowly began to pull it from her mouth. I fought the groan that bubbled in my throat.

I wanted to watch her wrap those pretty lips around my cock.

Her eyes never left mine as she chewed. I took my own bite before getting another for her. Giana opened her mouth again and I pressed the underside of the fork against her tongue. My cock was as hard as a rock, throbbing with need. I let out a shallow breath as I pulled the utensil from her lips. A small crumb was on her bottom lip. Setting the fork down, I lifted my hand to cup the side of her face.

Giana swallowed and I brushed my thumb across her lip, brushing away the minuscule piece of crust. "You had something on your lip," I explained, my voice hoarse and thick with lust.

I moved my thumb back to her lip, pressing down on it as I slowly dragged my thumb down. Giana wrapped her hand around my wrist. My eyes searched hers as I thought she was going to pull me away. Instead, she slid my thumb into her mouth. Her lips closed around me, sucking as she slid her tongue around me.

Jesus fucking Christ.

A low moan rumbled in my chest as my eyes settled on hers. Giana slowly pulled my thumb free from her mouth and released me. My chest rose and fell with every shallow, ragged breath I took. She moved off the seat, but instead of rising to her feet, she dropped down to her knees. She moved closer, pushing my legs apart as her hands moved to the waistband of my pants. I was entranced as she slid the button through the hole and dragged the zipper down.

She lifted her eyes to mine as she pulled my cock free from my pants and boxers.

My fingers slid through her silky hair. "What are you doing, princess?"

She wrapped her delicate hand around the shaft as a devious grin pulled on her lips. Desire danced in the blue depths of her irises.

"You'll see."

Opening her mouth, she slid my cock along her tongue, wrapping her lips around me. My hand gripped the back of her head. My head fell back against the seat, my eyelids fluttering shut as my face screwed up from the pleasure. She began to bob her head, pulling me to the back of her throat before sliding along my length until just the tip was in her mouth. I had wanted to feel her fucking me with her mouth and now I was getting everything I wanted.

It was like nothing I had ever imagined.

It was a million times better.

CHAPTER TWENTY-THREE
GIANA

The deck floor dug into my knees, but I ignored the pain as I watched the pleasure visible on Declan's face. His hands were in my hair, gripping the back of my head as I bobbed up and down, sucking his cock between my lips. I fought the urge to gag every time he hit the back of my throat. I couldn't get his entire length in my mouth, so I gripped the base with my hand and moved it with my mouth.

His body shifted beneath me, his hips involuntarily lifting as he drove himself deeper into my throat. I couldn't fight my gag reflex this time and choked around his cock. Saliva dripped from the corner of my mouth, but I didn't let go of him as I continued to move along his length. I stroked him with my hand and lips, swirling my tongue against him.

Declan's grip on my hair tightened and he went from pushing my head down on him, to abruptly pulling me away. I was left breathless, my lips swollen and my mouth agape as I stared up at him. A shadow passed through his hazy eyes and I could feel the tension rolling off his body in waves. He shook his head at me.

"I'm not going to last much longer if you keep sucking my cock like that," his mouth moved as he still held my head in his hands. "I'm not ready to come yet and when I do, I want it to be while I'm balls deep inside of that sweet pussy."

He stole the air from my lungs, his grip rough on my hair as he lifted up and pulled me toward his body. He released me as I began to move against him. His hands slid down my arms and my torso before gripping my hips. I moved my legs, planting my knees on either side of him as I straddled his waist.

Declan pushed my dress up to the bottom of my stomach before sliding one hand to grab my ass. His other hand was between my legs, pushing my panties to the side. Reaching down, I grabbed the length of him and positioned the tip of his cock against my center. My eyes met Declan's as I let go of his cock and linked my hands around the back of his neck. Dropping my hips, I slowly sank down onto him, taking the full length of him inside of me.

"Mmm, you take my cock so well, princess." Both of his hands were holding on to me, lifting me up and down as I used my thighs to push up. I rocked my hips, rolling them on him as I began to work my body against his. Declan's palm was soft against my skin as he moved one up to the back of my neck. His eyes practically rolled back in his head before he dragged my mouth down to his.

His tongue probed the seam of my lips and I instantly parted them, letting him in. His tongue slid against mine, soft like silk, yet urgent and fueled by the need burning between us. There was a passionate side to Declan. He savored every taste, every touch, and I reveled in the way he made me feel. Warmth was building in my body and I could feel a rush through my veins as he continued to top me from the bottom.

Abruptly, he pulled away from me and lifted me off his lap. He flipped me around, positioning me on my knees on the bench seat with my ass in the air. As he pushed my dress up to my waist, he hooked his fingers under the waistband of my panties and dragged them down to my knees. I held on to the top of the bench in an awkward position.

Declan trailed his hand up my spine. He wrapped one arm around my waist as he grabbed my right wrist with his other hand. Lifting it from the bench, he draped my arm over the back and pressed my chest against the top cushion. My arms were hanging over the side of the boat under the railing and I grasped for something to hold on to. I lifted myself up slightly, grabbing onto the metal rail.

A growl ripped through his chest, vibrating along my back as he nipped at my neck and rocked into me. I cried out in surprise, feeling the air pass through my throat without warning. I had no time for the shock of making a sound to settle in as Declan pinned me against the seat and began to piston his hips. His thrusts were harder, faster, driven by an insatiable need.

I wanted to fill every need he had.

Declan slowed down, his chest and the length of his torso pressed against my back. His hands were on mine, his palms pressed against the backs of my hands. Our fingers laced together, both of us holding on to the railing as he slowly stroked my insides with his cock. He peppered featherlight kisses along my neck and behind my ear. He was tender and soft. Gentle and attentive.

He shifted from racing to the abyss of ecstasy to taking his sweet time with me. The boat rocked with the ocean, the water lapping against the side of it. The sun was beginning to descend closer to the horizon. It wasn't quite dark yet and the clouds looked like wisps of cotton candy, stretching across the landscape.

I felt Declan's breath against my ear, his chest rumbling with another groan as he slowly rocked in and out of me. He whispered to me, but all it was, was air passing across my eardrum. I so badly wanted to know what he was saying.

One of his hands left mine. He gripped my chin, turning my head back to look at him. His eyes were a violent storm of emotion. Not a single one stood out as they all swirled together in the depths of his golden brown eyes. He stared directly into my soul, ripping me apart from the inside out. He stilled inside me.

"You were made for me, Giana," his lips told me. "I'm so lost in you. I swear, drowning never felt as good as it does with you." He paused for a moment, his lips finding mine in a haste as he thrust his hips again. "Get lost with me, princess. I don't want either of us to ever be found."

His chest was rumbling against me as he spoke. I read his lips while I felt the sounds of his words seeping through my skin. They vibrated in my bones, awakening my soul. I pulled my bottom lip between my teeth, not trusting myself to try and respond. I nodded, a ragged breath escaping me. Words would never do justice to the things I felt for him.

I couldn't tell him, I needed him to feel them. I needed him to know.

And the look in his eyes told me he did.

Flecks of green and brown meshed together. He stared at me like he truly saw me. And he did. Declan Parks was one of the only people who made me feel understood. Things were never complicated with him, they were always easy. He didn't expect anything from me except for a chance for him to show me he deserved me.

His eyes never left mine as he shifted his hips and began to fall back into a steady rhythm, stroking my insides. It wasn't long before I saw my name leaving his lips. He rocked into me harder. My orgasm was creeping up on me, blurring my vision. It spilled into my bloodstream, the pure ecstasy flooding my system as it hit me like a tidal wave.

I cried out, the ocean breeze carrying the whispers of his name across the sea. Emotion welled in his eyes and I didn't miss the way they glossed over. His grip on my face and my hand tightened. I clenched around him, my legs quaking as my orgasm tore through my body with enough force to rock me to the core. Declan thrust deeply into me once more as he came deep inside. His warmth filled me and his lips found mine in a haste as his thrusts slowed.

Declan released my face and leaned his forehead against my back. We were both left breathless, struggling to catch our breaths as he came to a stop. Together, we rode out the waves of our orgasms before he pulled out of me. I instantly felt his absence and I wanted him back. He pulled my panties back up, his cum dripping out of me.

His hands left me and I slowly turned around to look at him as he was fixing his pants. He stared down at me before dropping down onto his knees in front of me. I was sitting on the seat and he was pushing my thighs apart as he grabbed the sides of my face.

"I meant everything I said," he told me. The muscles in his jaw tightened momentarily. His eyes were dazed, but the emotion was still there, filling his golden irises. "I'm fucking drowning in your ocean."

My breath caught in my throat as I ran my fingers

through his hair. I swallowed roughly, feeling his words puncturing my heart like a sharpened arrow. His lips parted and he let out a soft sigh as he continued to stare into my soul.

"I love you, Giana Cirone."

CHAPTER TWENTY-FOUR
DECLAN

She looked so peaceful, so angelic and perfect, as she slept. Her eyes were closed and her lips were parted slightly. Her breaths were soft and quiet. I studied the way her face was so relaxed and innocent. There wasn't a single furrow of worry or wrinkle of the stress of life written across her expression. She looked just as ethereal as she did while she was awake.

There wasn't a single thing about her I would ever dream of changing. She was the literal definition of perfect. Perfect for me, at least. Sure, we all had our flaws, but they didn't mean a single thing when it came to Giana. I was hopelessly in love with her and it was one thing in my life I would never regret.

I slowly pulled my arm from under her head. I hated leaving her like this. I didn't want to leave her, period. I wanted to stay in bed with her for the rest of the day, but I had to get to my physical therapy appointment. Touching the side of her face, I gently trailed my fingers across her soft skin. Her eyelids fluttered open and she gave me a sleepy smile.

"Sleep, beautiful," I murmured as I tucked her hair behind her ear. I was half sitting up, half laying down. She lifted her head to look at me, wiping the sleep from her eyes. "I have to get to physical therapy."

She blinked her eyes open before glancing around. "Shit," she mouthed the word. She quickly twisted her body and I watched the way she moved. She was still naked from last night, and fuck. I wanted to bury myself inside her again. As she tapped on the screen of her phone, she quickly began to scramble out of bed. My brow furrowed as I watched her rise to her feet.

I followed after her, climbing out from under the blankets. She moved in a flurry around the room, finding clothes and pulling them on in a haste. I took my time and slowly dressed. Giana looked over at me with her eyes wide.

"I'm late for work," she signed to me, shaking her head. *"I'm never late. I was supposed to be there thirty minutes ago."*

My long strides closed the distance between us as I moved to where she was standing. My hands found her biceps and I looked down at her. "Breathe, princess. I'm sure no one cares that you're late."

She shook her head at me. "They're counting on me. We're short-staffed as it is."

"Giana." Her eyes moved from mine to my lips and back to meet my gaze. "What can I do to help?"

Her throat bobbed as she swallowed hard. I released her arms and her hands began to move along with her lips. *"My boss wants you to come volunteer, but he wants there to be publicity."*

My heart sank as I watched her expression transform into one that was filled with disappointment. Giana was the good in the world. She wanted the rest of the population to want to save the ocean of their own accord, not because someone in the spotlight brought attention to the work they were doing at the rehabilitation center. I knew her well enough to know that was exactly where her mind went.

"It could be a good thing, Giana. I know you hate it, and I do too, but we have to try and think of the positives here. It could bring in donations and even more people to the facility. That's the main goal, right? We need to educate the public one way or another, and we can't do that without drawing them in."

She contemplated my words. Her body visibly relaxed, the disappointment vanishing from her expression. She gave me a knowing look, one filled with understanding as she nodded her head. A sigh escaped her and she pursed her lips. *"I know. You're right."* She paused for a moment. *"Text me after your appointment and we can figure it out."*

I nodded and followed Giana into the bathroom. She handed me a brand-new toothbrush and I couldn't help but smile at the sentiment. After we stood side by side and brushed our teeth like a domesticated couple, she slid mine into the holder with hers and we both walked down to the kitchen.

Pausing, I turned to her and grabbed the sides of her face as I pulled her in for a swift kiss. It was quick and I knew if I let myself indulge too much, there was no way either of us were leaving. She tasted like mint and smelled like fucking heaven. I breathed her in before pulling away from her.

"I'll text you when I finish my appointment."

Her lips parted like she was going to say something but she abruptly closed them. She held both of her hands in fists with her thumb across her knuckles in the sign of an *S*. Crossing both of her arms in the shape of an *X*, she abruptly pulled them away from one another. *"Be safe."*

I stared at her for a moment, my mouth twitching. I wanted to know what she was actually about to say, but it was clear with her substitute. She wasn't ready to say it back to me and that was okay. I wouldn't want her to feel pressured or rush into anything. I wanted to say it to her. I wanted to tell her every goddamn chance I had, but I was afraid that would make her feel like I was forcing my feelings on her.

I pointed at her and formed a *Y* with my right hand and shook it as I winked at her. *"You too."*

I left Giana standing in the kitchen before leaving her house without another word. The air was thick and the moisture was palpable. I looked up at the clouds, the sun burning brightly in the sky. There was a thick haze. We were getting into the days where storms were predicted daily. The sky looked angry already with the threat of an impending thunderstorm brewing.

Disregarding the pending weather, I hopped into my Jeep and drove across town to Gabriel's office. He was already waiting for me since I ended up getting there about ten minutes late, but he didn't comment on it. Gabriel knew I operated on my own time and I always had. Things always moved a little slower in my world for me.

Gabriel had me do a few exercises before calling me into a private room to talk. He sat down on one of the chairs and I took a seat on the recovery bed. Gabriel handed me an ice pack for my shoulder, as he did after every session.

"You brought my boat keys, right?"

"Oh shit," I mumbled as I forced my hand into my pocket, hoping they were still there. Much to my luck, they were and I pulled them out and gave them to him. "Thanks again for letting me borrow it last night. I promise I didn't crash it or ruin it at all."

Gabriel laughed. "I would hope you're a little more mature than you were ten years ago."

Ten years ago, when I was just sixteen, Gabriel let me take his boat out with some friends. In my defense, it was a mistake on his part for letting a bunch of kids take out his most prized possession. Needless to say, it didn't end well when I ended up running it into the dock.

I narrowed my eyes at him. "You said you were never going to bring that up again."

"Bring what up?" He gave me a sheepish smile. "So, I think we're ready to discharge you, Dec. You've made tremendous progress and in my expert opinion, your shoulder appears to be strong enough for you to get back to surfing."

I stared at him for a moment, a little shocked by his words. I knew we were nearing the end of my treatment, but I wasn't expecting him to tell me this today. I thought I would have at least another week or so. Part of me was so excited to get back to doing what I loved to do, yet there was part of me that felt my stomach sinking.

"Already? Are you sure it's not too soon?"

Gabriel's eyebrows pinched together and he tilted his head to the side. "Do you not feel like you're ready to surf again?"

"I mean, I do," I quickly rushed the words out. "I just didn't think you would be discharging me this soon."

He nodded in understanding and then smiled. "Well, today is your lucky day then."

Was it really? I just told Giana I would start helping at the rehabilitation center and now I was going to have to tell her that I was going to be moving back to the West Coast.

"You have your entire career waiting for you. You're free to get back to doing what you love." Gabriel rose to his feet and pulled the ice pack from my shoulder. He held his hand out to shake mine. "It's been a pleasure working with you, Declan. I don't want to see you back here again, though."

I forced a smile onto my face. His words weren't meant to be cruel. If he saw me here again, it was because I was injured. I didn't want that to happen any more than he did. "I'll try not to come back again."

"You're always more than welcome to pay me a visit, just not on company time."

"Noted," I replied with a nod as I got up from the bed. "Thanks for helping me out. I really appreciate it."

"That's what I'm here for."

After saying goodbye to Gabriel and his staff, I couldn't help but feel an overwhelming sense of guilt. As I walked out into the parking lot, there was a text from Mark about needing to reschedule our lesson this afternoon. I quickly responded and told him the time change was fine with me. Then, I found Giana's name. I stared at it, unsure of what to say. I couldn't tell her through text that I was going to have to leave soon.

I didn't want to leave already, but there were constantly competitions going on and I had already missed so much time on the water. I needed to get back to it. The standings were constantly changing and if you wanted to stay on top, you had to be on top. I was no longer in that position and needed to work my way back up to where I was before I got injured.

And that meant I would need to leave within the next few days. The sooner I got back home, the sooner I could get back to doing what I needed to do. Although, the more I thought about Malibu, the less it felt like home. So much had changed in such a short amount of time. My mind was a clouded mess.

I knew one thing, though. I needed to tell Giana and I had to tell her in person.

CHAPTER TWENTY-FIVE
GIANA

As Declan sat down on the couch next to me, I couldn't help but feel like there was something that wasn't quite right. There had been a strange shift between us and the air was uncomfortable and incredibly stuffy. I stared back at him, my hands folded in my lap as my eyes desperately searched his. The walls felt like they were closing in on me. The anxiety that tore through me was suffocating.

After his physical therapy appointment earlier today, he had texted me and I wasn't sure if he would come see me at work at the time. He ended up not coming, instead opting to see me afterward. He was a little shorter with his words than normal and I could sense something was off by the way his messages came across. I imagined his tone would have been clipped and curt.

He told me we needed to talk.

That sentence alone was enough to have my anxiety heightened and it left me feeling unsettled.

He sat facing me, his hands clutching a water bottle. The silence was deafening, and that was saying a lot from someone who lived their life in silence. I hated it. I needed him to say something—*anything.*

"What's going on, Declan?"

The honey swirled in his golden brown irises. His throat bobbed as he swallowed roughly, and I watched him twist the cap from his water bottle and take a sip of it. He turned back to face me. "I was cleared to surf again. My sponsors have been calling, looking for an update. I haven't told them yet, but as soon as I do, they're going to want me back."

My stomach sank. I knew this day was coming—we both did. I just wasn't sure how it was going to affect me. *"You're going to have to go back home."*

He nodded slowly, a mixture of remorse and sadness mixing in his eyes. Leaning away from me, he set his water bottle on the coffee table and reached for my hands. His palms were soft and warm and he stroked the backs of my hands with his thumbs. "That place isn't my home anymore," he said, his lips carefully shaping the words that escaped him "My home is wherever you are."

"How soon will they want you to go back to the West Coast?"

"Most likely as soon as I can get there." He paused

for a moment. "With all the competitions I've missed out on, they're going to want me back in the water as soon as possible."

My heart split in two and the contents spilled out onto the couch, encapsulating both of us. My sadness mixed with his and it hung heavily in the air. A soft breath escaped me as Declan lifted his hand to cup the side of my face. I leaned against his palm, my eyelids fluttering shut as I reveled in his touch. I wanted to memorize the way his hand felt against my skin. The way he smelled. Everything about him.

I slowly opened my eyes to look at him again. A burning sensation pricked my eyes but I refused to let the tears break free. This was it. This was the end. Everything was crumbling around me. It felt like my world had come to a screeching halt. How could I have let myself be so delusional? How was I not prepared for this?

Because I went and fell in love with him.

"I wanted to tell you before I called my sponsors. I don't want this to end, Giana, and I don't expect you to give up everything you have here to move across the country with me."

A lump was lodged in my throat. My soul was shattered into a million pieces. There was a part of me that knew if Declan asked, I wouldn't hesitate. He was the love that set my soul on fire and I would have given everything up for him in a heartbeat.

"I would never ask you to stay when you need to go back to California."

His gaze burned into mine. His lips parted but he quickly shut them. I wanted to reach inside his mind and pluck out the words he was keeping to himself.

"We can make this work, princess," he assured me as he closed the distance between us and cupped my face with both of his hands. "I know long-distance relationships are never easy, but I can't lose you. I won't lose you."

I tilted my head to the side as his words seeped into my bones. I thought he was here to say goodbye, but he surprised me. It was the opposite of what I was expecting. *"We can still see each other whenever we get the chance."*

"I'll fly back here every chance I can to see you." He let out a ragged breath. "You're mine, Giana. I'm not giving you up. If you want me to give it all up, I'll do it. I'll stay here in Orchid City and never leave."

"I won't ever ask you to give up your surfing career for me."

A shadow passed through his expression. His jaw tensed and he nodded. "I know."

"When are you going to call your sponsors?"

"I don't know." He shrugged. "I have to sooner rather than later, but there was something else I wanted to talk to you about." Panic instantly flooded me and Declan could sense it. "The rehabilitation facility. Since I won't be here to volunteer, I want to sponsor a charity event for it."

My eyes widened as they traveled from his lips to meet his gaze. My brain wouldn't work to form words. My hands refused to work and my mouth was hanging wide open. We had always done small charity events that never really generated a lot of donations or attention. Having someone like Declan sponsor an entire event could be life-changing for us.

"I want to make it an annual thing. I'm sure it's probably too short notice for us to have it at the actual facility, so I called my brother and he suggested Orchid City Golf & Country Club. Since he is a member, he put me in touch with the president there. They had another event scheduled for this weekend, but it ended up being canceled."

My brain was struggling to process all of the words he was speaking. I could read his lips, I could understand everything he was saying, but my mind was almost in a state of shock. *"How? How did you do all of this already?"*

A smile pulled on his lips. "That's why I didn't stop by to see you today, princess. I ended up having impromptu meetings and had to work through all the details. I spoke to your boss and he is on board with the entire thing." He paused for a moment, wiping a tear from my face I hadn't realized had fallen. "They are going to host a golf outing on Friday and then we will have the actual charity event on Saturday. I ran into

Malakai when I was at the country club and he wants to sponsor the golf portion of it. He reached out to Nico and the Orchid City Vipers want to be involved."

"How are they going to get people to come? It's not an event without people attending."

"They already had people who signed up to golf and with the connections everyone has, it's going to take nothing to draw in the right people." His eyes were trained on mine, a ghost of a smile dancing across his lips. "These are the kinds of people you want. They are all loaded and just looking for another tax write-off."

"Declan," I whispered his name. His eyes widened at the sound and I ignored the self-conscious feeling that threatened to flood me. I never spoke. I couldn't even remember the sound of my voice. I wasn't even sure if the voice in my head was what my voice actually sounded like, but in that moment I didn't care. I couldn't stop myself. Lifting my hands, I signed to him. *"This could be life-changing for the entire facility."*

"I know, princess. We're going to get you guys the help and funding you need."

Tears fell from my eyes without warning and Declan caught every single one with his fingers. He brushed them away, his touch delicate like the wings of a butterfly. *"I don't even know what to say. I feel like saying thank you doesn't even begin to cover it."*

He shook his head and his smile reached his eyes. "You don't have to say anything, Giana. Let me help you. Let me do everything I possibly can." He caught the last tear and wiped it away. "I hope you have a nice dress for the event on Saturday, because I'll be needing a date."

I smiled back at him, feeling borderline giddy. My mind was still struggling to process it all, and I didn't have a dress. I needed to get one, and I would have to call Winter and Harper to see if they wanted to go shopping. *"What can I do to help?"*

"We've got it all covered. Maybe if you could just get some informative things together about what you guys do that we can share with the guests?" His fingers grazed my skin as he tucked my hair behind my ears. "The rest of your team is constructing a presentation, so anything you can add to that would be great. The most important part is your presence. That's all I really require."

The sadness still lingered in my heart at the thought of him leaving. I couldn't help but feel like this was going to be his send-off. He wanted to try long-distance and to make it work. I couldn't help but feel like I was signing myself up for a heartbreak, even though it was far too late to prevent something like that from happening. My heart was going to break whether we ended things now or later. Long-distance never worked—why would it be any different with us?

"Why are you doing all of this? You could have just gone back to your life and forgotten you even volunteered to help at the facility."

A soft chuckle rumbled from Declan's chest and his

gaze was filled with love as he stared back into the depths of my soul. "Because this is what you're passionate about, Giana. This is what you pour your heart into."

His eyes glimmered.

"And you are my heart."

CHAPTER TWENTY-SIX
DECLAN

Walking around the ballroom, I couldn't help but be amazed at how well things turned out. The room was already regal and elegant, but they were able to enhance its features in the most subtle ways. The chandeliers hung above with their sparkling lights. Lighting was altered and set to a lower tone with blue hues dancing throughout the room—the same shade as the ocean. Silverware shimmered from the tables with their massive centerpieces made from orchids, lavender, and baby's breath.

The golf outing yesterday went off without a hitch. They already had people who signed up for the outing that was canceled, so the small shift in charities was nothing. We couldn't have asked for better weather or a better turnout. And everyone seemed to follow suit to show up to the follow-up event this evening.

Nico and Harper were seated at one table, along

with a few other players from the Orchid City Vipers. The professional hockey team's general manager showed up and so did their coach. It was crazy, the different types of people and the amount of money that was walking around the room. I waved to them as I walked past, continuing to do my rounds to make sure things were in order.

Malakai and Winter were at another table. I didn't recognize the people they were seated with and Kai seemed less than interested in any of them. Winter was talking to another woman next to her who had the same midnight-colored hair. They looked similar and I figured they were related in some way. Kai's eyes met mine and he nodded in acknowledgment before dragging his bored gaze to the old man talking beside him.

As I came to a stop around the outskirts of the tables, I glanced around the room in amazement. I could not believe the entire place was filled with people. There was a DJ playing music in the far corner and a few people were dancing on the dance floor that was set up. I wasn't sure I was going to be able to make this happen for Giana, but together, we all did it.

Turning back around to face the door, I watched as it opened, momentarily frozen in place as Giana stepped through the threshold. The air left my lungs in a slow, tortured breath. Her light pink dress hugged her curves from her chest to her hips before it flowed around her legs, the bottom brushing against the floor. She looked absolutely ethereal. Her hair was long and curled, flowing down her back with two braids on the side, connecting in the back.

Her ocean blue eyes caught mine across the crowd and I watched the amazement in her eyes as her face lit up. She glanced around before focusing solely on me. My feet carried me across the room to her and I didn't stop until I was directly in front of her. Lifting one hand, I gently caressed her waist. My other slid beneath her chin as I tipped her head backward.

"You look absolutely enchanting," I murmured for her only, my lips moving for her to read them. "You're breathtaking."

"Thank you," she signed, a soft smile pulling on her lips as she mouthed the words. *"This is incredible, Declan. I cannot thank you enough for doing this."*

My gaze was lost in the depths of hers. The music coming from the speakers switched into a slow song void of any lyrics. Just the melody drifting from string instruments. "You can thank me by dancing with me." I withdrew my hand from her chin and gently wrapped it around hers.

Her eyes searched mine, slightly wide and a little frightened. She shook her head. *"Surely there's another way to show my gratitude."*

I tilted my head to the side. "You don't want to dance with me?"

Her lips parted and a soft breath escaped her. *"It's not that,"* she said, moving her mouth with the words. *"I don't know how to. The music... I can't hear the melody."*

Her admission damn near broke my heart. I slid my fingers through hers, lacing them together. "Do you trust me?"

Giana nodded. *"Yes."*

"Come with me, princess," I told her as I pulled her along with me. I looked back so she could read my lips. "I'll take care of you."

Giana didn't hesitate as she fell into step beside me. I half expected her to completely turn down the idea, but she surprised me as she moved out onto the dance floor with me. The last thing I wanted was for her to ever feel insecure. I never wanted her to feel like there was something she was unable to do. If there was anyone who could conquer the world, it was Giana Cirone.

Other couples were moving on the dance floor, circling around one another as they swayed to the slow melody filling the room. It was louder than I anticipated and I couldn't help but smile, knowing we wouldn't need words. It was almost as if we had our own nonverbal way of communicating. That and reading lips was a game changer.

Giana had taught me so much in the short amount of time I had known her. I never expected someone to change my life quite like she did. She blindsided me. She came out of nowhere and turned my world completely upside down. And I knew then I never wanted it to be the way it was before her again.

I would gladly look at the rest of the world upside down if it meant I could see her right side up.

Leading her toward the middle, we were shielded by others who were dancing around. Giana turned to face me and slowly inched closer as I guided her to my body with my hand. Her steps were deliberately slow, like her insecurities were holding her back. She finally stepped up to me, our feet on either side of one another's.

I slid my hands around her waist, flattening my palms against her lower back. She lifted her delicate arms, linking her hands behind my neck. "Follow me, princess. Just move your body with mine." I paused as the music vibrated the floor beneath my feet. It was so loud, echoing throughout the room, I could feel it inside my bones. Cocking my head to the side, I stared down at her. "Can you feel the music?"

She nodded her head as her fingers played with the ends of my hair that touched the collar of my dress shirt.

"Let me guide you and just feel it. Let your other senses take control."

I began to move my feet, slow and steady, stepping as my body rocked side to side. My hands guided Giana's hips and she began to sway with me. Her body moved like a weeping willow—undemanding and alluring. I pulled her closer and she wrapped her arms around the tops of my shoulders as she pressed her head to my chest.

There wasn't anywhere else I would rather be than right here, in this moment, with her.

I knew in my heart I didn't want to go back to California.

Our surroundings faded away and I held Giana close as we swayed to the entrancing melody of the orchestra playing through the speakers. Her scent invaded my senses. She was everything, consuming me. I was completely captivated and swept away by her. Everyone around us ceased to exist. Giana was the only thing I saw, the only one who truly mattered.

I loved her so much, it hurt, but it was the greatest, most magical pain I had ever experienced. I knew if things were to end between us, I would be a shell of a person after her. She was the one who had the power to destroy me. She held my heart within her two delicate hands and if she wanted to give it back, I wouldn't accept it. Giana Cirone could break me into a million pieces and I would still love her until my last dying breath. In this life and the next.

She was the abyss where the ocean met the sun.

As the song came to an end and the music switched to an upbeat tempo, we lingered for a moment longer. Everyone around us broke apart and began to dance faster. Giana slowly lifted her head away from my chest and took a step back. She didn't release me, as her hands clutched the back of my neck. Her head tilted backward, her ocean blue eyes clashing with mine as I held her hips within my hands.

"I love you, Declan."

The oxygen was drained from my lungs. My breath caught in my throat as the soft sound of her voice slid across my eardrums like the finest silk. She spoke. She spoke the words out loud *for me*. They weren't meant to be heard by anyone but me. Her voice was barely above a whisper, slow and tender, yet I heard every single syllable loud and clear.

I had hoped she would eventually say them back to me, but I never imagined she would do it this way. I wasn't sure I would ever hear the sound of her voice and, my god… it was the most delightful thing I had ever heard before. There was never a more heavenly sound than the way those words sounded as they fell from her perfect lips.

I couldn't help myself as I pulled her flush against me. My face dipped down to hers, capturing her mouth with my own. I was overcome with emotion, overflowing with too many feelings, I couldn't dissect them. My tongue slid along the seam of her lips and she parted them, letting me in. We were melting together, two souls entwined together as I poured myself into her with an intimate kiss. I didn't care who saw us, because none of those people mattered.

Only Giana mattered.

And I was so gone for her.

She was it for me.

―――

As the night came to an end, Giana and I stood side by side as we said our farewells to the guests as they left. The total amount of donations weren't tallied yet, but it was easily over half a million dollars. There were quite a few people interested in sponsoring different parts of the facility. So many doors had opened for Giana and her team tonight. It was like a fever dream and a dream come true for her.

Hand in hand, we headed out into the night air, walking through the parking lot to our cars. As we reached Giana's, I paused outside of the door. She turned to face me and my stomach sank as I realized I needed to be honest and up-front with her.

Her eyes desperately searched mine. *"Is everything okay?"*

"I spoke to my sponsors... They were pretty adamant that I get back to Malibu immediately." I paused for a moment, watching her face transform from the bright, carefree expression she wore all night to one laced with sadness. "My flight leaves tomorrow around noon. I just got the message while we were in the middle of the event that they had booked me on the first flight they could get me on tomorrow."

Her slender throat bobbed and her eyes grew misty. She pulled her bottom lip between her teeth and nodded. *"Well then, I suppose we had better make the best of the time we have left together before you leave."*

"You're not mad?"

Giana shook her head as she frowned. *"We knew this*

was coming, I just thought we would have more time. We will make it work, though, right? We can both visit each other."

"Of course we will make it work. I told you, I'm not losing you, Giana." I paused for a moment, reaching for her hand. "We will talk every day and visit every chance we get."

Her expression was laced with pain, desperation, and love. *"Will you come stay with me tonight?"*

"There's nowhere else I would rather be than with you."

Her eyes searched mine with a look I'd never seen before. For the first time since she walked into my life, she looked at me like she didn't believe me.

And why would she?

I was leaving tomorrow... and she wasn't coming with me.

CHAPTER TWENTY-SEVEN
GIANA

I watched Declan as he pulled his suitcase from the trunk of my car. It felt strange to think about the fact that he was leaving. He would be thousands of miles away from me instead of only fifteen minutes. I didn't want him to go, but I knew he couldn't stay. He had commitments he had made before I came into his life. I would never ask him to give any of that up for me.

He had left his Jeep at his brother's house and said his goodbyes to him and everyone else last night at the charity event. I hadn't seen the final numbers of how much money had been raised, but it wasn't really important to me in that moment. The only thing I could think about was, I was going to have to say goodbye to him in a few short minutes.

It was busy outside of the airport with people moving about in all different directions. Declan moved his suitcase onto the curb and closed the trunk before turning back to face me. A sad smile took shape on his lips and he extended his hand to me.

"Walk me in?" he asked as he stared at me with his eyes filled with emotion. I couldn't quite pinpoint what exactly was flashing through those golden brown eyes, but whatever it was, it was pulling on every damn string in my heart.

I nodded, slipping my hand into his as he grabbed his suitcase and we began to walk inside the airport. We fell into step beside one another, weaving past people until we made our way over to where Declan needed to check in and drop off his bag. Releasing his hand, I stood back and watched in silence as he moved through the line.

My heart had already sank into my stomach and I couldn't fight the feelings of despair encapsulating me. My mind diverted back to one of the darkest points in my life... the day my mother left this world. I couldn't help it. She was the one person in my life who left me without a choice. There was a sense of being abandoned by Declan. But deep down, I knew that wasn't the case.

I quickly shoved those thoughts from my mind. It may have seemed like he was leaving me by choice, but I was encouraging him to go. It was just as conflicting for him as it was for me. I could see the sadness in the features of his face. Neither of us liked this one bit.

Declan got through the line and left his bag before joining me where I was standing. With his ticket in one hand, his other found mine and we walked over to where the security lines began. I couldn't walk him to his gate. This was as far as I was allowed to go. This was where we had to say goodbye and go our separate ways.

"I hate this," he said as he released my hand. He tucked his ticket into his pocket and cupped both sides of my face. "Tell me to stay and I will."

A lump lodged in my throat and I wanted to tell him to stay. God, I wanted to so badly, but I knew I couldn't. I shook my head at him. *"I can't do that, Declan. You have commitments you already made."*

"Fuck it all. I'll give it all up for you. Right now, Giana. None of that matters."

He was breaking my heart and he wasn't even breaking up with me. If he kept pressing, I was going to cave. I was going to beg him to stay with me.

"We're going to make this work," I assured him, even though I didn't feel very optimistic about our arrangement. *"We will talk every day and visit each other whenever we can."*

He stared back at me, his expression unreadable. "I know. I just hate the thought of being away from you."

"I don't like it either, but this is how things have to be right now. We'll figure it out. We will make this work. I'm not against moving to the West Coast. I'm sure they have somewhere I could work there."

Declan shook his head. "I refuse to ask you to give up everything you've built here to follow me." He paused, letting out a ragged breath. "You're right. We will figure it out. I just need to get through these tours I've agreed to and then I'm coming back for you, princess."

"Don't make rash decisions because you're feeling emotional about this."

"It's not a rash decision," he insisted as he stepped closer to me. "My life is with you, not out there."

The line for security began to back up farther and Declan was going to be late getting to his gate if he didn't leave now. I wouldn't have put it past him to intentionally miss his flight right now. He couldn't do that, though. His sponsors were expecting him. They were counting on him, and that was how he got paid.

"Fuck," he breathed the word and I felt it across my face. "I have to go, princess. I really don't want to."

"I know, but you have to." I paused, reaching for his waist. *"FaceTime me later?"*

"As soon as the plane hits the fucking ground." His face dipped down to mine, our lips colliding with one another's. He kissed me slowly, with sadness and pain. My heart was breaking in two, but this wasn't goodbye. We would see each other again.

Releasing my face, he pulled back and looked down at me. "I love you, Giana. So goddamn much."

"I love you, too."

"I will call you as soon as I can," he assured me, his hands lingering like he didn't want to let go, but he did. He took a step back and it already felt like there were miles between us. "Fuck. I miss you already."

Jesus. My heart splintered and I fought back the tears that pricked my eyes. *"I love you. Have a safe flight."*

He let out a sigh, his shoulders hanging in defeat. "I'll always love you more."

With those final parting words, he turned away from me and headed into the direction of the line for security. I couldn't bear it. I couldn't stand there and watch him as he was leaving. Spinning on my heel, I all but sprinted through the airport, not stopping until I reached my car. And only after I dropped down into the seat, did I allow myself to cry as I left my heart in the airport.

And the tears showed no signs of stopping.

———

"You look like absolute shit," my brother spoke the words and signed to me as I opened the door to him and Wes standing on the other side of it. I was surprised he didn't just barge in like he normally did and decided to text me to let me know they were there. He also knew I was upset after dropping Declan off at the airport.

I gave him the middle finger and stalked back through the house until I reached the nest I had built for myself on the couch. Nico and Wes followed behind me. I was thankful for my permanent hearing loss in that moment. I could simply ignore them by just looking in the opposite direction.

They both sat down on the other side of the sectional, blocking my view of the TV with where they were sitting and I was laying. After dropping Declan off, I cried my way home and became a permanent fixture on my couch, watching sad romance movies.

I didn't want happy stuff. I just wanted to wallow in my sadness.

"Is this what you've been doing all day?" Nico inquired, and Wes looked between the TV and me.

I shrugged. *"So, what? Am I not allowed to be sad?"*

Wes elbowed my brother. "Cut her some slack. You'd be a damn mess if Harper left for one single night."

"We are apart when she doesn't come to away games with me." Nico narrowed his eyes at Wes. "And I wouldn't leave her to go *live* on the opposite side of the country."

His words struck a nerve and I abruptly shot up into a seated position on the edge of the couch. *"He didn't want to go. I told him he had to."*

Nico scowled. "And he listened to you?"

"I insisted. I refuse to have him give up his life for me."

Wes smiled at me. "You really are one of the most selfless people I've ever met."

"And stubborn," Nico added. His chest deflated as he let out a sigh. "I know you don't want him to give it up for you, but did you ever consider that maybe things changed for him now?"

I stared back at my brother. *"I know they did, but that doesn't mean he needs to throw it all away right now. We're going to make it work. We're going to visit one another and talk every day."*

"How long until that's not enough for either of you?" Nico asked me, his expression soft and warm. "I think I know what you're doing, G."

I tilted my head to the side. *"And what is that?"*

"This is your way of protecting yourself. If things go south, there's already distance between the two of you. You think it will make things hurt less if they don't work out."

"Shit," Wes mouthed before looking at the TV as his exit from the conversation.

I swallowed roughly as my brother saw right through me. He knew me better than anyone else and he just confirmed the one thing I had been keeping to myself this whole time. I never spoke the words to anyone yet he just simply knew it... because he would have done the same thing.

"What if they don't? I've never felt this with anyone else before... and I don't think I could handle losing someone else."

"I know it still hurts from losing Mom, but people aren't inserted into our lives to eventually leave us." My brother's eyes were filled with concern. "You've already let him in, G. It's too late now. I can tell from the way he is with you—he has no intention of leaving you. And if he does, I'll break his fucking face."

My brother's protectiveness earned the first real smile from me all day.

But I couldn't argue with a single word he said.

I couldn't protect my heart when it didn't belong to me anymore.

CHAPTER TWENTY-EIGHT
DECLAN

My feet were steady on the board and I bent my knees, bracing myself to keep my balance as my board drifted across the surface of the water. The air coming off the ocean whipped past me and the wave curled into the perfect barrel. Adrenaline coursed through my veins as I rode the swell, staying ahead of the crest crashing down behind me. It chased me through the water but it never caught up to me.

As I came out on the other side, I rode the surfboard closer to shore, letting the water push me in. I hopped off as I got close enough. The cool water rushed around my legs and my feet sank into the granules of sand. The Pacific Ocean was a stark contrast to the Atlantic.

It used to feel like home, but it just didn't feel the same anymore.

I had only been back in California for a week and it

had already felt like I had been back for months. It was strange how time distorted when you were longing for something that wasn't there. Talking to Giana wasn't as satisfying as being in her presence. I missed her touch, the way she smelled, the way she writhed in pleasure under my fingertips.

I fucking missed her more than I ever missed surfing.

Grabbing my board from the water, I walked across the beach, over to where I had left my belongings. It was early in the morning. I came out to watch the sunrise and surf before it got crowded. There were two other surfers in the water, but I paid them no mind. I just didn't feel like my normal self anymore. It was hard to pick apart the mix of emotions that had me on a constant roller coaster.

I set my surfboard down in the sand and took a seat on top of it as I stared out at the sea. The sound of the waves crashing against the shore bounced off my eardrums. I shifted my weight. I was restless and wanted to crawl out of my own skin. It was a strange sensation, not something I was accustomed to. Gone was the carefree Declan. The one who coasted through life without a care in the world.

I just felt... empty and lost.

Like a boat in the ocean without its anchor, without its compass.

Reaching into my backpack, I pulled out my phone and opened my text messages. Giana never texted me first, as she always waited to hear from me because of the time difference. I hated it. It was as if we were living two separate lives, on two separate planets. It was taking everything in me to not say fuck it all and hop on the next flight to Orchid City.

This was a lot harder than I had imagined it would be.

Giana didn't want me to give everything up for her, but she didn't realize that she *was* everything.

DECLAN

> Good morning, princess. How's my
> favorite girl this morning?

It didn't take long for Giana to respond and I couldn't help but smile and chuckle to myself as I read her question.

GIANA

> Me or Pop-Tart?

That damn turtle. I never imagined I would have gotten attached to a wild animal, but I had no one to thank but Pop-Tart for bringing me to Giana. Had I not found her on the beach, I didn't know if I ever would have stepped foot in that facility. Not that I didn't care about the work they were doing, but there was no need for me there.

Not that I had ever known.

DECLAN

> You. You're my only favorite, although
> Pop-Tart is a close second.

The small bubble with three dots popped up in the bottom of the screen and I patiently waited for Giana to type out her response. We had been FaceTiming every day and texting in between our calls. I was still working with Mark on my ASL lessons, but at this point, he thought it was becoming a little pointless.

After spending so much time with Giana and communicating with her and watching the way she communicated, I had picked up on a lot. We were able to have our conversations fully in ASL without me having to speak the words aloud. Every now and again there were a few words or sentences that would trip me up and require a little extra thought, but other than that, I had no trouble signing with Giana.

GIANA

I'm good. I'm a little tired because I was up late talking to a certain someone.

The smile on my face was a permanent fixture since Giana entered my life.

DECLAN

I don't regret a single second of that. And I'll keep you up tonight again, if you'll let me.

GIANA

You can keep me up as late as you want, whenever you want.

My smile faltered. The conversation was light-hearted, but it felt heavy in my soul. We shouldn't be stuck and limited to just our texts and video calls. I was struggling to find a free day that I could fly out there to see her. My sponsors were keeping me busy, as I had a lot of missed time I needed to catch up on. I managed to stay on top in the standings, but it didn't take much to slip out of first place.

I wasn't sure I cared about being on top anymore.

GIANA

> Pop-Tart is also doing well. Her flipper is fully healed. We're just waiting on her to pass a few more health clearances and then we will be scheduling her release.

Another thing that weirdly hurt because I knew it pained Giana. She wasn't ready to release the turtle back into the wild out of fear of what might happen to her. Giana wasn't afraid of the other animals in the ocean—she was afraid of the ones who walked the land and continuously poisoned Pop-Tart's habitat.

My phone vibrated as a picture came through of the faint scar that was left on her flipper. It amazed me, the work they were able to do. I walked into that facility with a bleeding, injured turtle, unsure of what the outcome was going to be for her. They managed to fix her up and heal her to the point she could safely be released back into the wild.

DECLAN

You are the most amazing person I've ever met.

GIANA

I didn't do any of it. You can thank Crew, our veterinarian, for his amazing surgical skills.

There was a twinge of jealousy that bubbled beneath the surface. It was a foreign feeling, but when it came to Giana, she had awoken a lot of feelings I never experienced before. I knew Crew was just a coworker. He was no threat at all. Yet I couldn't help but feel jealous at the fact that he got to see her almost daily. He got to see her when I couldn't.

I refrained from typing out my feelings to her. There was no need and no place for them here. It was something I needed to just swallow down and push to the back of my mind. Giana was mine and no one else's.

DECLAN

I don't want to talk about Crew and his skills.

Giana texted me back immediately and I could imagine the scowl on her face.

GIANA

You have nothing to worry about with Crew... or anyone for that matter.

DECLAN

I'm well aware of that, princess. I know you're mine. I just miss you and it's starting to get to me.

I lifted my gaze back out to the ocean, knowing if she were sitting on the beach at this exact moment, she'd be staring at a completely different ocean. My mind was a complete mess. She had inched her way into my heart and infiltrated every fiber of my soul. I couldn't think straight, couldn't see straight.

All I could see was her.

GIANA

I know. This whole thing sucks and I just want to see you.

I wouldn't be able to fly into Florida for at least a month, unless it was literally for a night or two during the week. I contemplated it, I just wasn't sure I could even get away for that long—not with all of the different events I'd been having to attend. Next week, I'd be leaving to go on a tour with different competitions at various beaches around the world. I wasn't sure how I could make it work.

DECLAN

Come see me.

GIANA

You want me to fly out to California?

It made total sense. Even if she only came for the

weekend, we would still be able to have time together before I had to go on tour. I had a surfing contest this Friday, but it was local. It wouldn't take up much of my time since I only had to surf one day.

DECLAN

With my schedule, I don't know when I'll be able to fly to you. I'm literally fucking dying here, Giana. Please come stay with me, even if it's only for a night or two.

The three bubbles popped up and disappeared. My stomach sank. I was a fool to assume she would drop what she had going on just to come see me. I was the one who moved back here, after all. She may have told me her thoughts and insisted I didn't give it up for her, but I ultimately made the choice. I could have canceled my flight that day and I didn't.

My phone vibrated in my hand again. My heart pounded in my chest as I unlocked the screen and read Giana's message.

GIANA

Of course I'll come. Tell me when and I'll be there.

I smiled. My girl was coming to see me.

For the first time in what felt like forever, my soul felt like it was at peace.

CHAPTER TWENTY-NINE
GIANA

People were moving in all different directions around the airport, but as I walked to where the baggage claim was, I only had one person in my sight. Declan was standing to the left of the automatic doors that led outside. His hands were tucked into the front pockets of his shorts and his tousled hair was pushed away from his face. He stood there waiting for me and when his gaze collided with mine through the crowd, I watched his lips lift upward, breaking out into a bright grin.

My footsteps hurried, carrying me closer to him. I couldn't help myself as I broke out into a jog, pushing past people as I made my way to him. Declan began to stride across the short distance and we met in the middle of a group of people. His eyes were shining under the fluorescent lights and he lifted me into the air.

My arms were linked around the back of his neck and my legs wrapped around his waist. Declan's hands cupped my bottom and I looked down at him after hugging him tightly. His muscles were taut and I missed the way he felt. Closing my eyes, I inhaled his scent deeply, feeling it snake itself around my soul. He smelled like sunshine and the ocean.

I missed him so much, it almost hurt to feel him this close.

Sliding my hands around to cup the sides of his face, my mouth crashed against his. I could taste the sea on his lips and he inhaled me as his tongue slid against the seam of my lips. There was a tenderness in the way he kissed me, but it was consuming. It was filled with a deep longing need. Our surroundings ceased to exist. No one mattered except for the two of us right now.

Someone bumped into us, unsettling Declan's balance. A growl vibrated in his chest and he broke apart from me, carefully setting me on my feet before pressing his lips against my forehead. There was almost a part of me that couldn't believe this was real life. I couldn't help the feelings I had of uncertainty, like maybe we wouldn't meet again as we had both agreed.

But here he was, standing right in front of me in the flesh. My hand found his, almost in a panic. He looked down at me and the damp tips of his hair brushed across his eyebrows. A wave of guilt passed through me. I was supposed to fly in late last night so I could watch him surf this morning, but I couldn't find a flight until today. He came straight to the airport after he was finished with his competition.

"I'm so glad you're here, princess," he said as he dropped my hand and signed the words. I smiled, not only at his words, but at the way his hands moved with swift precision. The fact that he learned ASL for me still shook me to my core. It was the greatest gift he could have given me. He had it set in his mind to master the language and seeing how far he had come with it filled me to the brim with pride.

"There isn't anywhere else I'd rather be," I signed back to him as my smile matched his.

He slid his hand back into mine and we went over and grabbed my bag as it made its way around the baggage carousel. Declan carried it out to his Jeep that was almost identical to the one he had at his brother's house. After loading it into the trunk and helping me in, he dropped down into his seat behind the steering wheel and whipped the vehicle away from the airport.

We drove through the city before ending up on the outskirts of a small town. It was along the coast and Declan drove down a winding road before pulling up in front of a small house that overlooked the ocean. I turned to look at him and he gave me a small smile as he put the car in park. "This is where I live."

I climbed out of the car and stared at the beautiful cottage-like house with the sprawling ocean behind it. It was a breathtaking view and I was lost in the awe of its beauty. As I watched the waves crash against the shore,

I noted the Atlantic almost seemed calm in comparison to the way the waves broke here.

Declan stepped up beside me, holding my suitcase in one hand. He looked over to me and my eyes met his. I missed the way the honey shimmered in the brown hues of his irises.

"It's absolutely beautiful here."

He stared at me for a moment, his expression unreadable. "It is, but there's something missing."

I tilted my head to the side as my eyes gazed into his. *"What could possibly be missing here?"*

"You."

I swallowed roughly over the lump that lodged itself in my throat. I was rendered speechless by one simple word. Declan slid his hand into mine, once again, and pulled me along with him as he led me inside his small house. It was almost like an optical illusion when we stepped inside. Everything was open, one room flowing into the other. It was clean and mostly bare except for a few paintings of the ocean hanging on the wall.

It was soft, minimalistic, and simple. Just like Declan. He was a man of few needs. I appreciated his simplicity and the fact that he just existed without putting too much stress on himself with the expectations of life.

He gave me the tour of his place and set my bag down on the floor in his bedroom, which made my heart do a little pitter-patter inside my chest. Rather than leading me back through the rest of the house, he turned to face me, his hands finding my hips before dragging my body flush against his.

Lifting one hand, he slid his palm along the side of my neck before pushing his fingers through my hair to grip the back of my head. He tilted it backward as his face dipped down to mine. His lips collided with my own and he stole the air from my lungs as he kissed me deeply. It was a kiss filled with need and urgency. It felt like a century had passed since the last time we were intimate. I craved his touch as if it were the last drop of water left on the planet.

With perfect precision and rushed movements, Declan stripped me bare, leaving both of our clothing on the floor before he lowered me down onto the mattress. Following along with me, he crawled across my body on the bed, settling between my legs. His hands were in my hair before trailing across every inch of my body. His lips were melting against mine and he shifted his hips as he slowly slid into me.

It was slow and torturous in the sweetest possible way. I stretched around him, moaning into his mouth as I accommodated the length and girth of his cock. Lifting my legs, I wrapped them around his waist as he began to thrust his hips, sliding in and out of me slowly. The urgency had dissipated and instead, he was taking his time.

No words were needed between us. We were lost in the moment, lost in one another. Our other senses took precedence. Touch, smell, taste, and sight. It was amazing how when you were lacking in one sense, the others were that much more heightened. I shivered under his touch as he slid his tongue along the column of my throat before trailing kisses along my flesh.

He smelled like the salt from the ocean and I inhaled deeply, reveling in his touch as he trailed his fingers beneath my breasts. He circled them around my nipples, his lips still moving along my throat and under my jaw. As I opened my eyes, I watched the way the muscles in his shoulders rippled as he braced himself and began to thrust harder into me.

His lips found mine once more. He tasted like a mixture of mint and sunshine. My tongue slid against his, soft like silk, and we were tangled together, melting into one. Sex with Declan was one of the most intimate experiences of my life. He poured his love directly into my soul and I absorbed every last drop of it. I trusted him with every fiber of my being. If there was one person that would never hurt me, it was this man.

Declan breathed against my lips, his breathing growing more shallow and ragged as he rocked into me harder. His lips left mine and he abruptly slowed his thrusts as he stared down into the depths of my soul. I was lost in the swirling golden hues of his irises.

"I love you," he whispered the words into my heart.

My breath caught in my throat. "I love you."

His eyes widened slightly as the words I spoke aloud slid across his eardrums. I watched his expression transform as a tidal wave of emotion encapsulated him. His eyes were soft and warm, his eyebrows slightly pinched as his nostrils flared. Declan swallowed roughly, his throat bobbing as he let out a ragged breath.

He collapsed against me, burying his face in the crook of my neck as his hand slid along the side of my torso. My arms wrapped around his shoulders as he slid one of his own around the back of my neck and held me close. His other hand was beneath my ass, lifting it up enough to get a deeper angle as he began to thrust into me once more.

Warmth was building in the pit of my stomach. My legs were wrapped tightly around his waist, my nails digging into his shoulders as I held on to him. Declan shifted his hips, moving faster and harder with every thrust. His chest vibrated against mine as he let out a low moan. He was everywhere, surrounding me as he consumed me. I was so lost in him.

Declan thrust into me again, sending me over the edge. I cried out, holding on to him with desperation as my orgasm tore through my body. The warmth spilled into my veins, spreading through my body like wildfire. I held on to him as he rocked into me once more before losing himself deep inside me. Another growl rumbled in his chest, vibrating through me.

His breath was soft against my skin and he peppered kisses along the top of my shoulder and up the side of my neck as his thrusts slowed. We were both left breathless and he lifted his face to look down at me. His eyes probed mine and his breath skated across my skin. We were both riding out the highs of our orgasms, left in the aftershocks of it. Ever so gently, he pulled out of me and I immediately felt his absence.

Declan got up from the bed and disappeared into the bathroom before returning with a washcloth. He was silent as he cleaned me up and slowly lowered himself back onto the bed beside me. His arm slid along my shoulders and he pulled me flush against his side. I settled into him, breathing him in as I rested my head against his chest.

I could stay like this forever, right here in this moment with him, but it wasn't our reality.

I slowly lifted my head, my eyes meeting his as I began to move my lips. *"Is there any way you can come back to Orchid City next weekend?"*

Declan tilted his head to the side. "What's going on next weekend?"

"We're releasing Pop-Tart into the ocean. I thought maybe you would want to be there for it."

A wave of sadness washed over his face and regret washed over his eyes. "I'm supposed to surf in a competition in Hawaii next weekend."

Dejection radiated from him and threatened to pull me into the depths of it. It slid through my soul and I tried to push it away, as far from my mind as possible. I couldn't show my disappointment, not when he was already feeling guilt for his absence.

"It's okay." I smiled at him in an attempt to assure him it was in fact okay. I never expected him to put anything before surfing. *"I just thought I would ask, but it's no big deal at all."*

Declan stared at me, his expression unreadable. I waited for him to say something, but he didn't. Instead, he pulled me close and rolled me onto my back as his lips found mine with urgency. This was what our reality was now: a series of missed events and borrowed time. He kissed me until I couldn't breathe, his hips shifting as he slid into me again.

He engraved his love into my soul and buried his remorse deep inside my heart.

CHAPTER THIRTY
DECLAN

Giana's time with me here had come and gone and she was already back home… without me. It felt like I picked her up from the airport and blinked my eyes and it was time for her to fly back to Orchid City. It was lonely here. I didn't have her, and I didn't have my brother. It just felt extremely isolating. I was also in the habit of isolating myself recently. Anyone who invited me to hang out, I turned down. I wasn't in the mood for company unless it was hers.

Floating on my board, I let the ocean push me forward, before pulling me back. I'd been surfing for the past hour and decided to be done. I couldn't explain it. It was almost as if the sport had lost its luster. I didn't care about being in the spotlight or being on top, even though that was where I was used to being. The pressure had begun to feel like it was too much. It was crushing and suffocating.

I just wanted to float in the ocean and enjoy myself, whether I wanted to surf or not.

I didn't know what had happened to me in my time off, but I didn't even recognize myself anymore. Surfing was the most important thing to me before I injured my shoulder. It was all that mattered. I ate, lived, and breathed the surf life. Now, it just felt as if my heart wasn't in it like it once was.

As long as I still had access to the ocean, my soul was happy.

But it would have been happier with her.

In three short days they were scheduled to release Pop-Tart back into the wild. I couldn't help but feel an insane amount of guilt. I was supposed to fly out tomorrow night to Hawaii. The contest started on Friday morning. I was supposed to surf Friday, Saturday, and Sunday. The thought of not being there with them when they released Pop-Tart was killing me.

That damned turtle held so much weight over me, but it was more than that. She symbolized something greater. She was what had ultimately brought Giana and I into each other's lives. Without her, I wasn't certain we would have met—or at least not under those circumstances. I was invested in her healing journey and now I wasn't going to be there for the final send-off.

It didn't sit right with me.

After floating in the ocean for a few more minutes, I allowed the waves to carry me back to shore. The beach was already starting to fill up with people who were here for the day. I made my way through a few of the crowds to where I had left my things. Setting my board down on the sand, I sat down on it and reached for my phone from the front pocket of my backpack.

This had become a daily habit. I would go out early in the morning and surf and swim, and then sit on the beach and talk to Giana while she was on a break or had some free time at work. She left three days ago and it felt like the time between us stretched even farther.

I smiled to myself as I saw her text message. I read over it, of her telling me she missed me and hoped I was having a good day so far and to text her when I got out of the ocean. It wasn't enough. I needed to see her face. I was tired of just having the text conversations and the closest thing I got to really seeing her was through a pixelated FaceTime call. Tapping on the screen, my face showed up as it began to call her.

After a few rings, her face showed up on the screen, sending mine up to the corner in a small rectangle. She smiled brightly as soon as she saw me and I watched her as she set the phone down so she would be able to sign to me. Grabbing my backpack and moving it in front of me, I did the same.

"Hey you," she signed to me before pausing to adjust her ponytail. *"This is a pleasant sight."*

"The pleasure is all mine, princess," I responded with a wink. "How is your day going so far?"

She gave a small shrug. *"No different than the rest of my days. How is yours? How were the waves this morning?"*

Flipping my camera around, I picked up my phone and slowly gave her a panoramic view of the beach and the ocean. It felt surreal that she was just here with me a few days ago, staring at the same body of water. I flipped the camera back around to face me and set my phone where I had it propped up.

"It looks absolutely beautiful," she said with one of the most genuine smiles on her lips. It shimmered in her bright blue eyes.

"Not as beautiful as you."

I didn't miss the way she momentarily ducked her head in an effort to conceal the blush that spread across her cheeks. It was something I had noticed she did occasionally. It was an innocent, shy movement and it lit a flame in my heart. I loved these moments with her, when her vulnerability shone through.

"When do I get to see you again?" I asked her.

Giana pursed her lips. *"Well, this weekend doesn't work for either of us. Maybe in another week or two unless you end up having some time to come here?"*

I instantly regretted even asking but I couldn't help myself. I was not thriving here without her. "I will see what I can do. I'm not sure when exactly, but I will come see you."

I couldn't expect her to keep coming here to see me.

It wasn't fair to her and I didn't want this relationship to be one-sided at all. That wasn't how things were supposed to work—and I needed this to work. If long-distance was no longer an option for us, then it wouldn't even be on the table. I'd be wherever she was.

"Okay," she told me with a smile, but I didn't miss the wave of sadness that passed through her expression. It was killing her just as badly as it was killing me. *"It's not a big deal, Dec. We'll figure it out and just take it one day or week at a time. You have a full schedule and I don't expect you to disrupt that at all."*

She had no idea how badly I wanted her to. There was a part of me that wanted to tell her to do just that. *Please expect me to disrupt my schedule. Please expect me to schedule my life around yours.* I couldn't. I knew Giana well enough to know she would feel guilty, as if she were pushing me away from doing what I loved.

There were plenty of other ways I could do what I loved without traveling, without doing it professionally, and certainly without living on the other side of the country from her.

"All of Pop-Tart's tests came back great and we're on track for her release on Saturday."

"That's great." I nodded, once again feeling a twinge of remorse in my heart. I was supposed to be there. "So, you guys are all set to get her back out there. What time are you doing that?"

Giana took a sip of a bottle of water and set it down before she began to sign again. *"We were planning on doing it in the morning around sunrise. We're going to take a boat to take her out to deeper waters to release her."*

"Is that what you typically do?"

She moved her head up and down. *"It just depends. Sometimes we do it right off the shore and sometimes we take them out away from the coast."*

I nodded in understanding. "I'm sorry I can't be there."

"Stop." She tapped the side of her right hand against her left palm. *"You have other obligations. No one is expecting you to be there, and I told Pop-Tart,"* she added with a playful grin in an effort to lighten the mood. *"She's not mad."*

"Do you actually talk to her?" I asked her out of curiosity. I had only ever heard Giana speak twice before and that was only to me. From what I gathered, she didn't normally speak.

She shook her head at me. *"We have a way of communicating nonverbally. And I like to pretend she can read my mind or understand ASL."* Giana let out a breath and pursed her lips momentarily. *"Since I lost my hearing, the only people who have heard me speak was you and my mother. I don't remember what it sounds like and I'm afraid of what it might sound like now that I'm not able to hear it."*

Her admission nearly broke my heart into two. She went that long without speaking out of fear of being judged because of the sound of her voice, but you wouldn't even be able to tell she suffered from total hearing loss. Her voice was so soft, so quiet, I couldn't imagine it sounding the way she probably imagined it did. There was still a cadence in her tone.

"Your voice is the most enchanting sound I've ever heard, princess. I'm in love with the sound of you."

Her lips parted and if I wasn't completely focused on her, I may have missed the words she spoke aloud.

"I love you, Declan."

"I love you more."

She shook her head at me, the sound of her soft laughter snaking around my eardrums. I stared back at her, my eyes trailing along the column of her neck as her head tilted back. As she lifted her head back up, her bright blue eyes met mine and my heart felt like it was crumbling into pieces.

I was officially done with this. Long-distance was never going to work, not when the only way I could see her like this was through a goddamn phone screen. I knew exactly what I had to do. If Giana wasn't going to ask it of me, I had to make the decision myself... and my mind was already made up before I came back out here.

This wasn't where I belonged.

I belonged with Giana Cirone.

CHAPTER THIRTY-ONE

GIANA

When I got to the marina, Crew and Miranda were loading up the boat, along with a few other people who worked at the rehabilitation facility. Today was the day we were officially releasing Pop-Tart and it was a bittersweet moment. I paused when I reached the dock, my eyes scanning the horizon as the sun began to lift higher into the sky.

I moved out of the way as two guys came walking past with a container that had Pop-Tart inside. A sigh escaped me and my footsteps were light on the wooden dock as I followed behind them, making my way to the boat. There was a twinge of sadness sliding through me. Declan was supposed to be here for this.

He had prior agreements he couldn't dismiss. I told him it was okay, and I meant it. I promised myself I wouldn't dwell on his absence. There was no one at fault, it was just a matter of bad timing. This day was supposed to be about releasing an animal back into its wild habitat... not about me and my feelings.

I stepped onto the boat and signed good morning to the crew and my coworkers before walking over to Pop-Tart. They transferred her into an almost tank-like container that was built into the boat, most likely where they housed fish. There was enough water inside to keep her comfortable, but there was a touch of fright in her eyes as she stilled.

"I know you're scared," I whispered to her, my voice most likely inaudible to anyone within close proximity. Pop-Tart stared up at me with a watchful gaze, almost like she could understand me. "I'm scared too, but it will all be okay. It's time for you to go home now and this will all be over soon."

We were only supposed to be going a few miles offshore to release her, so it wasn't going to be that long of a ride out there. The preparation was taking more time than it would for us to reach our drop-off point. I glanced around, watching everyone as they were getting things into place. Miranda approached me with a soft smile on her face.

"We should be ready to go in about five minutes," she signed to me. *"How is she doing?"*

"She seems frightened, which is to be expected. They usually are when they're moved around like this."

Miranda nodded in understanding. *"I'll tell them to*

hurry things along. Find somewhere to sit, so you're ready to go when it's time."

"Okay," I responded with a smile and watched her as she headed off in the direction of Crew and the two other guys. After giving Pop-Tart one last glance and making sure she was okay, I walked around the boat and over to the side by the dock. The captain stepped into the helm of the boat and the engine roared to life. Even though I couldn't hear it, I could feel the vibration of it under my feet. The sound moved through my entire body and I turned back to walk to the bow of the boat.

The sun was hanging higher in the sky and the light it cast down shimmered across the surface of the water. I watched, mesmerized by the way it shifted in a slow, methodical way. The ocean was painstakingly beautiful. Closing my eyes, I inhaled deeply, letting the salty air tantalize my senses.

My heart clenched. It smelled exactly like *him.* Like sunshine and sea. His golden brown eyes drifted into my thoughts and I hung on to the memory of him. I was afraid for our future. There was a part of me that was sure this wouldn't last. Even though I tended to be more independent, being away from him was really taking a toll on me. I loved him, and the last thing I wanted was for things to end between us, but I wasn't sure how much more I could take of this.

It was weighing heavily on my heart.

The last I heard from him was when he texted me on

Thursday when his plane touched down in Hawaii. This was the longest we had gone without talking, except he had texted me a few times. There was a strange feeling of disconnect, like the space between us was growing. We were living two separate lives now. I tried to not focus on it too much but when I allowed my thoughts to drift in that direction, it nearly split my heart in two.

Soft fingers touched my shoulder and I turned around to see Miranda standing behind me. Her expression was unreadable and I tilted my head to the side as I raised my eyebrows in question.

"There's something you might want to see," she signed to me before abruptly turning away.

My eyebrows dropped and tugged together as she began to walk in the opposite direction. My heart clenched as a million worst-case scenarios raced through my brain. Was there something wrong with Pop-Tart? I was terrified something had happened that would prevent us from releasing her. It wasn't a done deal until that turtle was safely in the water.

Racing after her, I rounded the helm and almost ran directly into her back as she stopped along the dockside of the boat. I let out a ragged breath and stared at the back of her head. Miranda glanced over her shoulder at me, a ghost of a smile playing on her lips as she raised her hand and pointed out to the end of the dock that was touching solid ground. My gaze followed in the direction she was pointing and the air left my lungs in a rush.

I blinked twice in an effort to chase away the illusion, but he didn't dissipate. He didn't vanish into the salty air like a mirage. Declan Parks was standing at the end of the dock, staring directly at me.

I couldn't move. I was frozen in place. My heart clenched, my throat constricted. I couldn't fathom a single coherent thought and before I knew it, my body was moving involuntarily as I climbed over the side of the boat and onto the dock.

Miranda didn't try to stop me and I wouldn't have let her if she had. Declan was jogging toward me, his footsteps rattling the wooden planks beneath his feet. I broke out into a sprint, racing to him. The ocean air whipped my hair around my head. He was all I could see. I couldn't get to him fast enough. We connected and crashed into one another.

His hands gripped the sides of my face and our mouths collided. He tasted like *him*. He had to be real. My hands grabbed his biceps and I held on to him. Tilting my head back, the kiss deepened. His tongue slid against mine, soft like silk. God, I missed him so badly it was fucking ripping me apart.

Abruptly, I broke apart from him. My eyes desperately searched his. He blinked. He was here. He was real. I wasn't dreaming. This wasn't an illusion.

"Declan," I whispered his name, my voice shaking around the syllables.

His expression was soft and warm and I watched the wave of emotion as the sound of my voice entered his ears. "Fuck. I missed you, princess."

"What are you doing here?"

I didn't even bother stopping myself. The words tumbled from my lips. The vibration in my throat felt foreign and I pushed away the self-conscious thoughts of not being able to hear my own voice. My brain wasn't functioning properly and I simply spoke without any inhibition.

"Don't ever hide your voice from me," he said before his face dipped down to mine. His lips met mine in a gentle caress before pulling away again. "I could listen to the sound of you and nothing else for the rest of my life."

My throat welled with emotion so thick it felt like it was going to close. "You're here."

He smiled brightly. "Yes, I am, princess. I'm here for good."

I tilted my head to the side in question as I tightened my grip on his arms. "How?"

"I'm done, Giana. I got to Hawaii and realized I couldn't do it anymore. I'm tired of the distance between us, I'm tired of missing time with you." He paused for a moment, a ragged breath escaping him. "I pulled out of the competition and told them I'm done."

His words penetrated my soul. I shook my head at him, my brow furrowing. "What do you mean you're done?" I whispered.

"You didn't want me to give everything up for you, so I didn't." He stopped for a beat and the smile never fell from his lips. "I gave it up for me because I can't live without you, Giana. I refuse to live a life where I can't see you every day, where I can't touch you whenever I want to. Where I can't smell the lavender and vanilla scent of your shampoo. Where I can't hear that sweet fucking voice of yours."

The sun cast its light across his face, illuminating his gold-tinged eyes.

"I'm home, princess."

CHAPTER THIRTY-TWO
DECLAN

G iana stared back at me like I had hung the sun in the sky. Her eyes grew misty and she let out a soft laugh as she shook her head in disbelief. She practically jumped onto me, wrapping her arms around the back of my neck as she pressed her body flush against mine. Her lips brushed my ear.

"I'm so glad you're here."

Jesus. The sound of her voice. It was literally everything. I could die right here on this dock and I would die the happiest man in the universe. The way she spoke, it did things to me I could never explain. You never knew how badly you were missing something until you had your first taste of it. I had a taste of her voice and I wanted every single sound she would give me.

"Me too, princess."

My heart clenched in my chest while warmth

flooded my veins. I was overcome with emotion—so much more than I anticipated. I never wanted to be apart from her again.

Giana released me and took a step back as she slid her hand into mine.

"I suppose we should probably get on the boat, huh?"

She smiled brightly and it reached her eyes. They glimmered like the ocean beyond us. She led me along with her until we reached the side of the boat. Everyone on board was waiting for us and I didn't miss the grins they were all fighting to conceal. I helped Giana on before hopping on after her. We found a spot to sit on one of the bench seats and the captain pulled the boat away from the dock.

Releasing Giana's hand, I wrapped my arm around the tops of her shoulders and pulled her against my side. She settled against me, resting her head against the side of my chest. Leaning into her, I buried my face in her hair. My eyelids fluttered shut and I inhaled deeply. Her scent invaded my senses and soothed my soul.

Lifting my head, I propped my chin on the top of her head and stared out at the ocean as we coasted out into the open waters. Giana was right where she belonged, tucked against me and under my arm. This was exactly where I was supposed to be.

I struggled with the urge to fly here instead of Hawaii, but I tried. I went there for the competition, but as soon as I boarded the plane, I wanted off. I knew I had made a mistake but at that point, I was stuck. As soon as the plane landed, I texted Giana to let her know I made it there safely, but I couldn't get the feeling to go away.

It didn't take much for me to cave. I never made it to my hotel. I never even left the damn airport. I reached out to my agent and sponsors immediately and told them I couldn't do it. Not a single one of them were happy with me and I was sure I was now on the top of their shit lists, but it didn't matter. I waited for hours in that damn airport until I could get the next flight to Florida, which wasn't easy to find, considering the layovers I had.

I didn't bother stopping back in California before flying straight here. And I didn't let Giana know because I knew she would try to talk me out of it. There was something about her that I wasn't able to refuse and if she would have insisted I stayed for the competition, I would have just to appease her.

She wanted me here. It was written all over her face. I could read it in her body language. She just didn't want to be the reason I gave everything up, so that was why I made the choice to do it for me. For what I wanted. And it just so happened to be her that I wanted.

I still needed to make arrangements to put my house on the market. I needed to pack and move my stuff as well. Hell, I wasn't even sure about where I was going to stay, but I was sure my brother would let me stay at his place if Giana didn't want me with her. I knew it was a lot happening at once, but sometimes I didn't think things through before I did something.

My dream had always been to start a surfing academy. I loved teaching others and seeing the joy on kids' faces when they first found their balance and could master standing upright on a board. It felt like this was my destiny. Leaving my surfing career to start a new one was the best move I could have made, even if I didn't have the plans mapped out.

I had time.

We finally had time.

The boat slowed to a stop after we were about two miles offshore. Giana lifted her head away from me and rose to her feet as the captain killed the engine. I followed along with her and we walked over to where Pop-Tart was in her container filled with water. I looked down at the turtle, feeling a smile pulling on my lips. Who would have thought an injured sea turtle would have brought the one thing that was missing into my life?

"Who wants to do the honors?" Crew said as he glanced between all of us.

Giana turned to look at me. *"I think you should be the one to release her... since you were the one who found her and saved her life."*

I smiled at my girl and shook my head. "I think we should do it together."

Giana's smile matched mine. *"I like that idea."*

Together we both maneuvered the turtle out of the container and walked to the back of the boat. There were two steps that led to a smaller platform that was only a few inches above the surface of the water. I held most of Pop-Tart's weight as I lowered myself down to my knees and Giana did the same.

I looked at the water below before looking at Giana. "Ready?"

She nodded. "I'm ready," she whispered the words, so soft and quiet, no one heard them but me. They weren't meant for anyone but me.

Gently, we both lowered Pop-Tart down into the water, dipping her beneath the surface before letting her go. We were both on our knees, side by side, as we watched the turtle move her strong flippers as she began to swim through the water. She turned around to face us, almost as if she were saying goodbye before she began to dip deeper. We watched her until the distance grew and we couldn't see her any longer.

I looked over at Giana, seeing the tears falling down her cheeks. Reaching for her, I pulled her close against me, wrapping my arms around her. "It's okay," I murmured as I held her close and stroked her hair. She couldn't hear the words I spoke, but it didn't matter. She could feel them. "She'll be okay."

We stayed like that for a few minutes as everyone else began to get the boat ready to head back to the marina. Just like that, it was over. It was like turning the page and closing a pivotal chapter in both of our lives.

Pop-Tart was where she was supposed to be and she never would have had that chance without any of us on the boat.

Giana finally pulled away and let out a breathless laugh before pushing the tears away from her face. *"That was embarrassing,"* she signed to me as the engine of the boat came to life.

"Nothing you do is ever embarrassing. You're allowed to feel. You're allowed to express your emotions."

She gave me a small smile. *"I just cried about releasing a turtle into the wild. I've done this countless times and have never had it hit me this hard."*

"Pop-Tart was special."

Giana nodded. *"She really was. If it weren't for her, I'm not sure I would have ever found you."* She paused for a moment as her eyes penetrated mine. *"You're both home now."*

"We're both where we've always belonged."

"Are you moving back in with your brother?"

I shrugged and let out a chuckle. "I'm hoping. He doesn't even know I'm back yet."

Giana rose to her feet and held her hand out to me. I slid mine into hers and stood up with her. She let go of my hand and slid her arms around the back of my neck as she tilted her head back to look at me.

"Stay with me."

I could barely hear the words over the rumble of the engine, but I fucking heard them. My eyes widened slightly and bounced between hers. "Are you sure that's what you want?"

She pulled me closer, lifting onto her toes as her lips brushed my ear. "You're what I want."

A smile was on her lips as she moved back to look at me. She took a step away and offered me her hand again. "Come. Let's go home."

I smiled back at her as I slid my hand into hers and she led me up onto the main part of the boat. I watched her as she stood along the side, staring out at the ocean. I couldn't tear my eyes away from her. I was completely entranced by her.

And I was home.

EPILOGUE
DECLAN

One Year Later

Giana eyed me skeptically from the passenger seat as we got into my Jeep and I started the engine. I couldn't help but grin at the feisti-ness that was rolling off her in waves. She wasn't one for surprises, so when I told her I had one for her when she got home from work, she was less than amused. It was killing her, not knowing what I had in store for her.

And sitting on this surprise for the past month had been killing me as well.

It was a short drive to Orchid Beach Marina. Only about four minutes, to be exact. We could have walked but I didn't want to push my luck with Giana before we got to the best part of the night. She gave me the same sideways look as I parked the car and turned off the engine. Giana didn't even wait for me to walk over and open her door.

She moved in a haste, pushing it open and hopping out. Laughing softly to myself, I shook my head and climbed out of the Jeep and made my way over to her. She was standing beside the car with her arms crossed over her chest as she glanced around the marina with a touch of curiosity in her eyes.

And then she pinned her gaze on me and shot daggers at me.

I stepped up to her, reaching for her arms before pulling them away from her chest. "You really don't like surprises, do you, princess?"

She pursed her lips and narrowed her eyes at me in response. She refused to physically speak a single word to me. The last real surprise I had for her was when I flew in from Hawaii and showed up for Pop-Tart's release into the wild. She seemed ecstatic about that surprise.

Giana did tell me she didn't want birthday surprises, but she never said she didn't want 'just because' surprises. I wanted to spoil her. I wanted to shower her with my love and give her everything she deserved and wanted.

"Well, get on with it already," she signed in a huff.

I tilted my head to the side. "Why do you hate surprises so much?"

She let out an exasperated sigh. *"I don't want to talk about it."*

"Not acceptable," I told her as I shook my head. "What happened?"

A wave of annoyance washed over her expression before a touch of sadness passed through it. *"When I was ten, my parents decided it was a good idea to throw me a surprise birthday party. I came home from the beach with my brother and when I walked in, everyone jumped up, yelling surprise..."* She stopped for a moment and gave me a knowing look before continuing. *"Naturally, I couldn't hear them and I wasn't paying attention, so I literally walked right into the house and into another room without even noticing anyone."*

My heart sank as I pictured her as a young child, having something so normal like that completely ruined. She had told me before that she was eight when she lost her hearing, so I was sure it was still somewhat fresh at ten, especially having a reminder thrown into her face that she couldn't hear.

"I'm so sorry, Giana," I breathed softly as I slid my hands up and down her arms. "I didn't know."

She shook her head. *"I was so embarrassed, but that wasn't the only time I was embarrassed with a surprise. When I was in high school, two girls who I thought I was friends with said the boy I had a crush on had a surprise for me out in the courtyard. They had me convinced he was going to ask me to prom. I walked out there, like a damn idiot, and found him making out with another girl."*

Well, fuck. I didn't know which surprise would have been more humiliating. They were both equally embarrassing, but the first was just an innocent one. The second sounded more malicious and was coated with ill intent.

"One of the girls walked up behind me and grabbed my shoulders, which scared me because I didn't know she was there. I screamed and got the attention of my crush and the girl whom he was making out with. The two girls spilled my secret to him about me liking him right then and there."

I couldn't help the anger that built inside me. It was clearly a decade ago that this happened, but I wanted to find this guy and put my fist through his face for hurting my girl. No one—and I meant *no one*—would ever get away with hurting her.

"I ran away like a coward, but Winter ended up giving one girl a bloody nose and the other a black eye." Giana smiled at the memory. *"She made it better, but after that last surprise, I absolutely hated them."*

"No more surprises," I promised her as I cupped the sides of her face. "After this one, of course, which I promise you will love."

She swallowed roughly. "I'm sorry," she whispered.

"You have nothing to be sorry for, princess. I'm sorry for how cruel people are, but I promise that will never happen to you again. I will always protect you. You're safe with me."

Her lips twitched. "I know."

I pulled her to me and pressed my lips to her forehead before taking a step away. I slid my hand against hers, lacing our fingers together before leading her down to the dock. We made our way down the main one, before stepping onto one that jutted out to the side. There were various boats lined up and I stopped in front of an off-white center console boat that had bright blue script on the side.

Giana's brow furrowed and she looked over at me as she released my hand to sign. *"This isn't Gabriel's boat."*

I smiled and shook my head. "No. This one is yours."

Her eyebrows relaxed but her eyes widened as she looked at me in total shock. She glanced from the boat and back to me. Her lips parted and she spoke. "What?"

"The boat is yours, princess," I told her as I pointed to it. Her eyes scanned the side, stopping when they reached the name of the boat.

Poptart.

She whipped her head to look at me again. "You bought me a boat."

Jesus, I loved the sound of her voice.

"The ocean runs through your veins, Giana. I know it soothes your soul. On the water is where you are content. I figured you could use this for whatever you wanted, whether it be research or just because you need to get out there."

She stared at me. "You bought me a fucking boat and you named it Poptart."

A chuckle rumbled in my chest. "Yes. I bought you a fucking boat and she's an important part of our story."

"You're absolutely mad."

I grinned as I stepped closer to her. "Mad about you."

A string of soft laughter fell from her lips and she lifted onto her toes to kiss me. It was soft and tender, slow and sweet. She poured her love and emotions into me as her lips moved against mine.

Pulling away from her, I stared down into her ocean blue eyes. "I love you."

Our love was wide and vast like the ocean.

It knew no limits and it knew no bounds.

Her lips brushed against mine once more.

"Not as much as I love you."

EXTENDED EPILOGUE
DECLAN

Two Years Later

Sitting behind the steering wheel of our boat, I watched Giana in absolute awe. Her sage-colored bikini stood out in contrast against her tanned skin. It hugged her curves and I allowed my eyes the pleasure of trailing across the planes of her flesh. She was absolutely breathtaking and absolutely perfect.

There was no one else on this planet quite like her.

She paid no mind to me as I killed the engine, walking across the front of the boat. I rose to my feet and stalked across the space to her, closing the distance between us. I couldn't help myself. I couldn't keep my eyes off of her, and God knows I struggled to keep my hands off her body whenever she was within reach.

Giana turned to look at me, her smile reaching her eyes. I held on to her hips just as the boat shifted beneath us. I bought Giana the boat as a present two years ago, but she insisted it was our boat and not just hers. I wanted her to have access to the deeper waters whenever she pleased. We were both cut from the same cloth with the ocean embedded in our souls It was a part of us. It was where we belonged... *together.*

We came out frequently, whenever we had the chance. Giana had been busy lately with the expansion of the research facility. Richard had been able to generate enough donations and extra money that they were able to upgrade their facility and a lot of the equipment they had there. She had been so busy setting everything up and making sure things were in order and I loved her for everything she did.

Giana knew what she wanted in life and refused to let anything come between her and her dreams.

Since being back in Florida, I had opened up my own surfing academy. Even though the waves were mild compared to the West Coast or other parts of the world, it had a lot of appeal. There were a lot of people who were interested in learning how to surf. And in the months that tourists were here, business boomed even more with the surfboard rental service I offered.

I began to slide my hands along her bare skin on the sides of her torso. She was wearing a bikini with a cover-up tied around her waist like a skirt. Her skin was tanned from the sun and I fucking loved seeing her like this.

"What are you up to, Declan?"

A smirk pulled on my lips. Fucking Giana on the boat had become a favorite pastime of mine, but I didn't bring her out here for that today. Slowly pulling away from her, my lips shifted into a small smile. Giana's eyes matched the ocean and they widened as I dropped down to one knee in front of her.

She lifted her hands up to her mouth, covering it as her jaw fell slack. The small velvet box in my pocket felt like it weighed a ton. I wanted to pull it out, but there was something else I wanted to do first. Lifting both of my hands in front of me, I began to sign to her, not bothering to speak the words out loud as I split my heart wide open and bled out onto the floor of the boat around her feet.

"I love you, Giana Cirone. I've loved you since the first time I laid eyes on you, it just took a while for me to come to terms with it. And I didn't want to seem like a total creep with the whole 'love at first sight' thing... but that's exactly what it was. My soul knew yours and the moment I walked in that morning with Pop-Tart, I swear it felt like coming home."

I paused for a moment, smiling up at Giana as I watched silent tears fall from her eyes. I wanted to stand up and kiss them all away, but I couldn't. Not until I told her everything I needed to tell her.

"The time we spent apart was the worst time of my life. I can promise you that will never happen again. I'm yours, princess. I've always been yours and I always will be yours. My love for you is like the ocean. It's endless and its depths

are unreachable. You're not only my world, but you're my entire heart, Giana. Marry me. Spend the rest of this life with me. I want us to grow old together, to have little babies running through the sand and swimming in the ocean."

She dropped her hands away from her face, her lips parting as a ragged breath escaped her. A smile was spreading across her lips and she wiped the tears from her face in a haste. The sunlight danced in her eyes, shimmering like the surface of the ocean.

"Will you marry me?" I signed to her before grabbing her hand.

Her entire face lit up but her gaze penetrated mine with nothing but love. "Yes," she spoke the word out loud. It wasn't often that she spoke, but her voice was the most beautiful melody I had ever heard. She spoke directly into my soul. "Yes, I'll marry you, Declan."

A wave of relief washed over me and my vision blurred as I was overcome with a rush of emotions. Tears fell from the corners of my eyes and the sound of her soft voice echoed in my ears. Reaching into my pocket, I pulled out the small box and opened it before plucking the ring from it. It was white gold with a diamond in the center, shaped like a drop of water—like a drop of the ocean.

"It's beautiful," Giana breathed the words as I took her left hand in mine and slid the ring over her fourth finger. She stared down at it before her eyes met mine. I slowly rose to my feet and she lifted onto her toes as she snaked her arms around the back of my neck. "I love you."

"Forever, princess." I spoke the words for her to read my lips before brushing my mouth against hers.

"Forever," she echoed me before our mouths collided together, sealing the deal.

An eternity would never be enough time with Giana, but I would take whatever time I could get with her... in this life and the lives that came after.

Wherever she went, my soul would always follow.

A LOOK INSIDE THE
NEXT BOOK

Written in Ice is the third book in the Orchid City Series.
It is a hockey romance where he falls first that features
Weston Cole and a spicy romance author looking for a
new muse.

Continue reading for a look inside Written in Ice

CHAPTER ONE
CHARLOTTE

"We need something different from you, Charlie," my editor, Diana, said with urgency through the phone. I stared out of the second-story window of my Victorian-style house. The morning fog had settled in the air, casting a blanket across the sleepy, coastal town. "The market is shifting and I think it would be good for you to shift with it."

I slowly sipped my lukewarm coffee, tasting the bitterness on my tongue. "What are you suggesting?"

"You have a strong readership and following with the romantic thriller audience, but there has been a recent demand for contemporary." She paused for a beat. "We have an entire proposal for you, to have you write in this different genre under a pseudonym."

I snorted. "Diana. Do I really strike you as the type to write romance that doesn't involve some type of suspense or thriller aspect?"

"You're an extremely talented writer, Charlie. I don't think there is a genre you couldn't write."

I fell silent as I considered her words. I appreciated her positivity and the fact that she thought I was capable of more than I had been doing. The thought of writing outside of my normal genre made me slightly uncomfortable. I was comfortable in my little romantic suspense box. Not all of the books I wrote had romance in them, so it wasn't something I was super into.

"Where did this request come from?" I questioned her as I continued to stare out the window, watching the sun as it struggled to break through the thick fog.

"It came from my boss and when I suggested you for the job, they did not hesitate."

I chewed on the inside of my cheek and sat down on the deep windowsill. "I don't know, Diana."

"Tell you what—I'll send over the proposal. Take a day or two to look it over and I'll check back in with you in a few days to see if you've changed your mind. And if you do so before I reach out again, shoot me an email or give me a call."

"Fine," I agreed with reluctance.

I could hear the smile in Diana's voice. "That's not a no, so I'll take it. It will be in your inbox in a few. Talk soon."

She ended the call, leaving me alone with my now cold coffee and thoughts I wasn't certain I wanted to entertain. If the publisher had requested it, there was a need. Publishing worked like any other business—there was a chain of supply and demand. The market was demanding more mainstream romance. Would it be so bad for me to branch out into something I wasn't used to writing?

I looked out at my sleepy little town once more. Idyll Cove was where I had grown up, but it was also where I drew a lot of my inspiration from. It was the perfect setting with the perfect vibes for writing romantic thrillers.

How the hell was I supposed to draw inspiration from here to write something light and fluffy? Something without any type of mystery or suspense? It felt like such a mundane concept and the spark was not there.

My computer dinged as an email came through and I lifted myself from the windowsill as I walked over to my desk and set down my phone. Pushing out my chair, I didn't bother to take a seat as I opened up my mail and saw one from Diana. I stared at it for a moment with the pointer of my mouse hovering over the subject line. Curiosity had me tapping my forefinger down on the mouse, opening up the email.

And as my eyes began to scan the screen, my jaw fell slack. My eyes widened. My lungs momentarily failed while my heart pounded against my rib cage. I planted both of my hands on my desk as I read over the entire proposal again.

They wanted me to sign a four-book deal, one that centered on a small beach town. They had it all planned out, exactly what they were looking for, but they were still allowing me creative freedom. It wasn't even that part of the proposal that had me picking my jaw up from the ground.

It was the amount of money they were offering me. It was an advance I had never imagined seeing in my life.

There was no way I could turn a deal like this down. I pushed away from my desk and pulled my blonde hair back into a ponytail. I looked back at the screen again, feeling slightly panicked while also feeling a rush of adrenaline coursing through my body. I would be a complete idiot to say no.

Grabbing my phone from my desk, I began to pace as I typed in my brother's name and hit the Call button. He answered on the third ring, sounding slightly out of breath.

"Hey, Charlie," he said breathlessly. "Jas, I'll be right back. Keep working on our routine without me."

I looked at the clock on my wall and swore to myself under my breath. I didn't even bother to check the time before calling him. My brother was a professional figure skater who competed in solo performances and in pairs. He was training for the World Championships later this year.

"Shit, I'm sorry, Leo," I said with regret as I shook my head. "I didn't even realize the time. We can talk later, it's not that important. Just call me when you're done."

"Charles." He said my nickname he had given me when we were younger with a sternness that only an older brother would possess. "You're rambling. You only do that when it's something important. What's going on?"

My footsteps were light as I continued to pace around my office. I scratched the side of my head. "I just got this deal from my editor I don't think I can turn down but I don't know what to do because it's different from what I normally write and what if I can't pull it off?"

"Okay, just take a deep breath." He paused for a second. "I have another hour left on the ice and then I'll be over with some Chinese food. We'll look over it and figure it out, okay?"

I let out a ragged breath as I finally stopped moving. "Sure. Yes, that sounds good."

"Just do me a favor and try not to have a stroke or something before I get there."

I let out a choked laugh. "I'll try not to."

———

My brother showed up about an hour and a half after we talked on the phone. It felt like it took him three to get there. He found me sitting on the floor in the middle of my office with a pros and cons list, along with a whiteboard full of sticky notes with ideas.

Leo paused in the doorway, tilting his head to the side. He studied me for a moment and shook his head with a smirk before walking into my office and sitting down on the floor across from me. When I needed to think, it was where I felt centered and grounded. This was my best thinking spot.

I pushed my board to one side and my list to the other. He started pulling a whole buffet of containers of food from the bag he brought with him and spread them out between us. He handed me a pair of chopsticks before picking up one of the containers for himself.

"So, what do we have going on here?" He shoveled a scoop of lo mein into his mouth. "Are you plotting? Does that mean you've decided to accept the deal?"

I shook my head. "No. I still don't know what to do. I was making a pros and cons list and then random ideas started floating into my brain, so I needed to write them down."

"What exactly would the cons be?"

I swallowed a mouthful of rice and grabbed my water to wash it down. "I came up with two. Number one: I've never written contemporary romance and might not be able to. Number two: I need to temporarily go stay somewhere to research and write."

Leo lifted a questioning eyebrow. "Okay, fuck

number one. You can write anything. And number two... why can't you stay here?"

"Inspiration, Leo. Idyll Cove is perfect for what I've been writing. I need something new, something fresh. I need to feel the ocean, to capture the essence of the beach to write it into a story. To be able to craft an entire beach town."

"Go stay with Grams," he said with a shrug, as if it were the simplest solution. "She lives right near the ocean. It would be perfect for you."

"Grams has her own life. I doubt she wants me to come stay there, and for who knows how long." I paused and took another bite of my food. "I mean, it could be months or longer. It just depends on how long it would take me."

Leo rolled his eyes. "Please, Charles. You know she would love for you to come stay with her. She always wants us to come visit."

I stared at him for a moment, considering the option. It wasn't a bad one. Our grandmother lived in Orchid City, Florida. She was minutes away from the beach and it really was the perfect place to draw inspiration from. It ticked all the boxes I needed to check off. But still, there was hesitation within me. I couldn't help but question whether or not I was the right author for this job.

"Where's the proposal?" Leo asked, breaking through my thoughts. "Let me see it and I'll give you my real opinion."

I pointed over to my desk. "I have it pulled up already."

Leo stood up from the floor and carried his carton of food over with him to my desk. He dropped down into my seat and I watched him from where I was sitting as I continued to slowly eat the rice and vegetables inside my own container. He was silent, his eyes glued to the screen as they scanned the words that were written out in the document.

His eyes widened before his gaze quickly flashed to mine.

"Charlie... are you fucking kidding me right now?"

I swallowed roughly and shook my head. "That's what they sent me."

He blinked. "And you're seriously sitting here making a pros and cons list?" He shook his head with an incredulous look on his face. "You can't turn this down. This is too good of a deal. Hell, if you won't do it, I will."

Laughter spilled from my lips as my brother abandoned my desk and came back to sit across from me. "I'm not sure they would even want your grocery list."

Leo laughed and gave me the middle finger while he shook his head. His laughter trailed off and the expression on his face turned serious as he stared back at me. "This is life-changing, Charlie. I hope you realize that."

"I know," I said quietly as I nodded. "I'm just afraid I won't write it the way they want."

"Do not even entertain those thoughts. I believe in you. I know you are going to write the shit out of these little romance novels."

A soft laugh escaped me. "You're annoying."

He gave me a crooked grin. "That's what brothers are for."

ACKNOWLEDGMENTS

To my husband: I'll never be able to thank you enough for your never-ending support. You listen to me ramble about my ideas and offer solutions and answers (even if I don't want them). You're my best friend and I'm so thankful to have you as my biggest cheerleader (sans skirt). I love you forever x infinity.

To my entire team: Alex, Carol, Loren, Emma and Erica—you guys are absolutely amazing and I appreciate you all. You guys are so vital in every step of the way and I don't know what I'd do without you guys.

To my sensitivity readers: Cat and Honey —I can't thank either of you enough for your help and guidance while writing this. I appreciate you both and your knowledge with ASL and deaf experience.

To my editor, Rumi: You know how to make shit shine. I love you forever.

To my cover designer/bestie Cat: 637. That is all.

To my twin Cassie: Never hugs and always drugs.

To my momager LB: What the hell was I doing without you my whole life? Forever thankful for you. ILY

To my influencer team and review team: You guys

are seriously so amazing. I appreciate you all and your support never goes unnoticed!

To my author friends (I'm not going to list everyone, but you know who you are): We all know that sometimes this industry is toxic as hell. We all know that sometimes the people here want nothing but the worst for you. I cannot say that about all of you, though. The support, the way we all stand by each other. It's something special that I will treasure forever.

To my bookish friends (again, I'm not going to list because I'm bound to forget a name lol): All I have to say is I am so glad that books brought us together. You are an integral part of my life now and that means so much to me.

And last but not least, to my readers. You are all what keeps me writing. If you didn't show your love for these stories I create, there would literally be no point in me creating them. I will always be so grateful for each and every one of you. Seriously, I think I have the best readers out there.

ALSO BY CALI MELLE

WYNCOTE WOLVES SERIES

Cross Checked Hearts

Deflected Hearts

Playing Offsides

The Faceoff

The Goalie Who Stole Christmas

Splintered Ice

Coast to Coast

Off-Ice Collision

ORCHID CITY SERIES

Meet Me in the Penalty Box

The Tides Between Us

Written in Ice

STANDALONES

The Lie of Us

ABOUT THE AUTHOR

Cali Melle is a USA Today Bestselling Author who writes sports romance that will pull at your heartstrings. You can always expect her stories to come fully equipped with heartthrobs and a happy ending, along with some steamy scenes.

In her free time, Cali can usually be found living in a magical, fantasy world with the newest book or fanfic she's reading or freezing at the ice rink while she watches her kid play hockey.